Aruna's Journeys

Also by the same author:
The Moon Over Crete

Aruna's Journeys

Jyotsna Sreenivasan

Merryl Winstein, Illustrator

SMOOTH STONE PRESS
P.O. Box 19875 ◇ St. Louis, MO 63144 ◇ USA

For information contact:
Smooth Stone Press, P.O. Box 19875, St. Louis, MO 63144

Printed on recycled paper

Library of Congress Cataloging-in-Publication Data

Sreenivasan, Jyotsna
        Aruna's Journeys / by Jyotsna Sreenivasan

Summary: Aruna, an 11-year-old Indian-American girl, reluctantly visits her relatives in India and in the process discovers more about who she is.

ISBN: 0-9619401-7-4

[1. East Indian Americans--Fiction. 2. India--Fiction. 3. Women--India--Fiction.] I. Title.

Library of Congress Catalog Card Number: 96-92328

Acknowledgments

I would like to thank all the people who read drafts of this book and gave me suggestions and comments: my parents, Vimala and V.V. Sreenivasan; my husband, Mark Winstein; my sister-in-law (and illustrator), Merryl Winstein; my mother-in-law, Sharon Winstein; my brother, Sharad Sreenivasan; 12-year-old Nisha Sahay, the first kid to read the manuscript; Joe Kelly, publisher of *New Moon: The Magazine for Girls and Their Dreams*; professional editor Ellen E.M. Roberts; and Marilyn Courtot, publisher of *Children's Literature: A Newsletter for Adults*.

Note: There are Indian words in this book you may not be familiar with. Please look in the glossary at the back of the book for the definitions.

To my parents -- Vimala and V.V. Sreenivasan

Chapter 1

"Why do I have to go?" Aruna demanded. She banged her school books down on the kitchen table. "Why can't I stay home?"

"They will be expecting all of us," Mom explained. She calmly waved a stick of incense in front of a picture of Lakshmi on the kitchen counter. "And you are too young to stay home alone until late at night."

"I'm not young at all. A lot of other girls even baby-sit when they're 11. Anyway, I bet they won't even notice if I'm not there." Aruna watched the incense make a thread of smoke in the air. She had just walked in from school and was still standing in her sneakers even though she *knew* she was supposed to take her shoes off at the door.

"I cannot understand you, Aruna," Mom said. She finished waving and stuck the incense stick into a banana in front of Lakshmi. "You have been complaining that you have no friends at your new school. And now we are invited to the Vatsyas' house for dinner. You have a chance to get to know another girl in your grade, and you don't want to go!"

Aruna sighed. She couldn't explain to her mother why she didn't want to go. "I'll be outside," she said.

"Come home in time to get dressed to go!" Mom warned. "You can wear the new dress I made you."

Aruna slammed the door behind her. She looked up at the steely cold gray sky, and back at the barren dirt covered with straw around their house. They had just moved into this house built especially for them, and the grass hadn't grown in yet. Their house was one of the few that had been completed on the block.

Aruna was glad that from the outside of their house, no one could tell an Indian family lived there. It had light blue siding and a chimney, and it looked just like a regular American house. But inside the house, it didn't smell like hamburgers or cookies, the way normal American houses did. It smelled like incense, or fried spices.

Most of the street was bordered by plots of bare brown dirt, sometimes with large digging machines sitting on them. There were no trees around. Her chest felt heavy. She crossed her arms and shivered, and walked across the street to a pile of dirt in front of an unfinished house. She peered at the dirt and searched half-heartedly for any interesting new rocks to add her rock collection.

Aruna hadn't wanted to move at all. She had lots of friends at her old school. She'd been at the same school since kindergarten, ever since she and her family had come to the United States from India. And now she was in a new school, and the kids didn't seem very friendly at all.

Worst of all, there was another Indian girl in her grade — Sonal Vatsya. She didn't want to go to the Vatsyas' house and get to know Sonal any better.

Aruna had never had another Indian girl in her grade before. At her old school she had been the only Indian in the whole school, except for another girl a grade above her. Aruna had tried her best not to run into her. But at this school there were more Indians. Sonal was in a different home room but they had science and math together. So far Aruna had managed not to speak to her.

That's one reason Mom and Dad had wanted to move here — they wanted Aruna to meet more Indians and do more Indian things. Here, Aruna was going to have to go to "Sunday school." Except it wasn't at church, like normal Sunday school. It was in a junior high school building in the next town, and she would learn Indian dance and culture.

Aruna didn't like to call attention to the fact that she was Indian. She couldn't help the fact that she had brown skin and straight black hair and eyes so dark you couldn't even see the pupils. She couldn't help that she looked "foreign" and like she didn't belong. She hated it when her teachers asked her questions about India. She barely remembered India! How was she supposed to know whether people in India used elephants to carry logs? She had never seen anything like that.

So she certainly didn't want to hang out with another Indian girl and *really* make everyone notice she was different.

Aruna found some shale in the dirt. It was nice — perfect thin cool gray slices stuck in the mud, just starting to separate from each other. But she didn't pick them up. Shale was so common, and it didn't look nearly as exciting once you picked it up and the pieces fell apart in your hands.

The sky was starting to get darker. Aruna trudged back home as the fading light made the street look even more forlorn.

Chapter 2

"So this is Aruna!" Lots of brown Indian faces nodded and smiled at Aruna as she stood in the living room of the Vatsyas' house in her scratchy new lavender dress with puffed sleeves. She had lost the battle to wear jeans and a sweatshirt.

"How do you like your new school?" one woman with large gold earrings and red lipstick asked loudly.

"It's OK," Aruna said softly. She looked around the room and saw only adults — Sonal was fortunately nowhere in sight.

"Come and sit down here," a gray-haired woman offered. She patted the sofa beside her.

Aruna didn't want to sit by someone she didn't know, so she followed her mother and sat down beside her on a sofa. She accepted a glass of juice from Mrs. Vatsya. Aruna's dad was sitting in the family room with all the other men.

As she sipped her juice, she gazed around at the

grand, high-ceilinged living room. Mom had said the Vatsyas were rich: both of Sonal's parents were doctors. The room was decorated with heavy wood statues of Hindu gods and goddesses. Aruna saw Ganesha sitting on the carpet in the corner, his elephant trunk resting on his fat belly. Two or three large batik pictures adorned the walls, and a Persian rug with an intricate pattern was displayed under the glass-topped coffee table. In one corner was a grand piano.

Aruna's house was not this big, and they didn't have a piano or any big wood carvings. Aruna's dad was a professor of computer science. Her mom worked in a jewelry store part-time. Mom said they were not rich like the Vatsyas.

Suddenly, Aruna was aware of someone standing right beside her, and she looked up to see Sonal. She was a tall girl with short, curly hair, wearing a dress covered with lace and frills and bows.

"Here is Sonal. You girls go and play," Mrs. Vatsya said.

Aruna's heart sank, but she smiled at Sonal politely. She knew she had to spend time with Sonal this evening, but she didn't intend to *like* her.

Sonal grabbed a handful of salted nuts from the coffee table and said, "Come on, let's go up to my room."

They climbed a wide spiral staircase to Sonal's room and sat down on her bed. It was a canopy bed. Aruna looked up at the white lacy canopy, which matched the white lacy bedspread and curtains. The carpet was pale pink. There was also a white dresser with a gold-trimmed mirror, and a white rocking chair piled with teddy bears.

Aruna wondered how Sonal could stand all the whiteness and lace. Aruna had picked out a bright red carpet for her own room.

On the walls were posters of Martina Navratilova and Steffi Graf playing tennis. "Wanna see my trophy?" Sonal asked. She picked up a trophy with a gold figure of a woman tennis player on top and handed it to Aruna. "I won it at the club. I'm really good at tennis," she added, in case Aruna had failed to grasp that fact. Aruna admired the trophy and handed it back.

"D'you play tennis?" Sonal asked.

Aruna shook her head. "I don't know how. But I play soccer."

"*Everyone* plays soccer," Sonal said. She rolled her eyes. "I'm a forward. I scored the most goals ever on our team last year. How many goals have you scored?"

Aruna had to admit she hadn't scored any — not in real games, anyway. "Usually I'm a fullback," she explained. "Sometimes I'm a midfielder."

"Oh. That's too bad. You'll never get to score anything. Anyway, if you haven't found out already, the soccer team in your neighborhood is pretty lousy. I don't think they won even one game last summer! My team was the champion last summer. We have a really great coach — a man, and he shows us all these moves that usually only boys get taught. . ."

Aruna started to zone out as Sonal went on and on about her soccer team. Fortunately, just then Sonal's mom called them down to eat.

After they'd filled their plates at the buffet table, Sonal suggested they go back upstairs to eat and play video games. "I'm really good at video games," Sonal put in. "How many video games do you have at home?"

Aruna didn't have any video games, but she wasn't going to tell Sonal that. She sat down beside her mother and said she'd eat with the other women in the living room. Sonal sat down next to her. As they ate their pooris and curries off plates balanced on their knees, they listened to the women talk.

"So you got into medicine, Meera! Congratulations!" the loud woman with the big gold earrings was saying to a college girl in a pretty turquoise-blue salvar kameez.

"Thank you," said Meera. She smiled modestly at her plate.

"Your mother is so lucky. Both her children will be doctors!" Aruna's mom said. "I hope I will have the same luck some day." She looked at Aruna and raised her eyebrows. Aruna stared down at her plate and pretended not to hear. Aruna wanted to be a geologist, not a doctor, and Mom knew it.

"Meera and her sister are the perfect Indian children," said a very small, dark woman with a piercing, high-pitched voice. "Why can't all our children obey their parents like Meera? Why can't they be content to live at home while in college? What is wrong with home? What is wrong with parents?"

All the women nodded and murmured in agreement. Aruna hated to always hear how she was supposed to "obey her parents."

On the way home in the car, Mom asked Aruna, "How did you like Sonal? Is she a nice girl?"

"She's OK. She brags a lot, though." Aruna was glad she had a good reason not to like Sonal.

Dad laughed. "Her father brags a lot too. That's probably how she learnt it."

"Maybe you will find some friends at the Sunday school. It starts in a few weeks," Mom said.

Aruna wasn't sure whether she wanted to go to Sunday school and learn Indian dancing and prayers. Why couldn't her family just be normal and American so she didn't have to learn all these weird things?

Chapter 3

*A*runa stood on the corner of her street and twisted the hem of her T-shirt in her hands. She was trying to decide whether she should go knock on Amber's or Emily's door.

It was a cool, windy Saturday morning, and she had just wandered outside after watching a few cartoons. She turned the corner onto their street. They lived right next door to each other. She thought she might as well just walk by their houses. She didn't have to knock if she didn't want to.

Amber and Emily were two girls in her grade. Amber had long wavy red hair that she pulled back into a ponytail. She was a big, tall girl with red cheeks and freckles. Emily had straight dark brown hair with bangs, and blue eyes. They stood at the bus stop together every morning, and whispered to each other and giggled. A few times Aruna had stood next to them to join in their conversation, and they said "hi" to her. Once Emily had asked her a few questions about where she'd lived before she moved here. Aruna thought maybe she just had to try harder to be friends with them.

She stopped and squatted over a pile of gravel next to an almost-finished house to see if she'd find anything interesting. She had been collecting rocks for three years, since she was nine. She kept them in a box with cardboard dividers that created a separate space for each rock.

When they were moving Mom had wanted Aruna to get rid of her rocks. "Why do you want to carry that box of stones to the new house?" Mom asked. Aruna had ignored her mother and personally carried the box on her lap in the car as they drove to the new house.

She continued sifting through the gravel. A couple of years ago she had found a real, clear crystal growing out of a piece of gravel! At first glance she had hoped it was a quartz crystal — that would have been amazing to find a quartz crystal in a bunch of gravel! But it was much too soft — she could scratch it with her fingernail. Was it a gypsum crystal? She was never completely sure.

She didn't see anything very interesting in this pile of gravel, so she walked on. But soon after, she saw a pile of chunky black rocks. She bent over them and picked one up. She saw it was mostly a deep, dark, glossy greenish black, but she also saw some clear flecks that might be quartz and some goldish patches — mica. Maybe it was a granite made mostly of hornblende! She dropped it into her jacket pocket. She'd show it to Amber and Emily. That should get a conversation started. At her old school she always showed her friends the new rocks she found.

She continued towards Emily's house, still not sure whether she would knock. But as she got near, she saw Amber and Emily on the front porch steps. She stopped and waved to them. They waved back and called "hi," in a not very enthusiastic way. Aruna could tell they weren't that happy to see her. But she wanted some friends, so she walked up to them and took out the greenish-black rock she had in her pocket.

"Look what I found!" She held out the rock to them. "D'you like rocks?"

"Only the kind on engagement rings," said Amber. She peered at the rock in Aruna's hand. "It looks like coal."

Aruna wasn't sure what she meant by rocks and engagement rings. "No, it's not coal at all! Look — it's really a very dark green. That's hornblende! I think it's granite made mostly of hornblende."

"Wow, I've never seen a horny rock before," said Emily, and they both started giggling.

"Not horny, *hornblende!*" insisted Aruna.

They giggled even louder, and Amber said "A horny rock! That's a good one."

Aruna didn't understand why they were laughing. Was there something funny about "horny?" She couldn't ask her parents, because they knew even less American slang than she did. Maybe she'd find it in the dictionary.

She wondered if she should just pretend to understand the word and laugh also. But before she decided, Emily jumped up and said, "I'm freezing! Let's go inside."

Aruna watched Emily open the door. Then she asked suddenly, "You mind if I come in?"

Emily looked at Amber, then shrugged at Aruna. It wasn't a very hopeful sign, but Aruna followed them inside.

They went up to Emily's room and sat on the bed. Emily had a dresser with a huge mirror. The top of the dresser was cluttered with a blow dryer, combs and brushes, and head bands. Emily started talking about washing her hair.

" — and I just *had* to wash it last night or it would've looked cruddy today. I have to wash it every other day at least, and Mom said it was too late and she didn't want me up half the night running the blow-dryer and — "

Aruna didn't even own a blow dryer, and she only washed her hair once a week, on Saturday night, and then only if her mom reminded her. What was so great about washing your hair?

" — and I ran out of conditioner last night, and I just *made* my dad go to the store right then to get some more because my hair is so frizzy without the conditioner . . ."

Aruna started to wonder if she should get a blow-dryer or use conditioner. Emily made it sound very important.

"Oh, you have the new *Teen Talk*!" Amber snatched a magazine up from the floor. On the cover was a pale-skinned blond girl with very straight hair.

"She's who won their modeling contest," Emily said. They both inspected the girl on the cover. Aruna leaned over to look too. She hardly ever saw this magazine because her mom thought she was too young for it. "It's called *Teen Talk* and you are not a teen," Mom pointed out.

"She's cute," Amber agreed. "Not gorgeous, but definitely cute." She flipped through the magazine to read the article about the modeling contest. "Ohmigod! Guess how old this girl is!" Amber gasped.

"I know. Thirteen," Emily said. "She just made the age limit."

"She looks at least sixteen," Amber commented. "D'you think we'd look that old if we wore makeup?"

"Prob'ly. My sister says a lot of these models are not that great-looking without their makeup on. And speaking of my sister, wait till you hear this, Amber. I found out that she actually entered this contest! She actually sent a picture of her ugly self to *Teen Talk*!" Emily screeched and pounded the bedspread. "I just laughed in her face when I found out."

"Your sister's really pretty, Emily!" Amber protested. "And you look just like her. I hate you both, you're so gorgeous! I wish I didn't have these splotchy red cheeks and freckles. I can't wait till Mom lets me wear foundation so I can cover up my horrible skin!"

Aruna looked with alarm at Emily to see how she was taking Amber's confession of hatred. But she just smiled and went over to her tape player and turned it on. "I just got the new City Boys tape."

Amber and Emily stood up and started swaying and snapping their fingers in time to the music. Aruna knew it wasn't polite to stare at them, so she trained her eyes on the pages of the magazine. She didn't know how to dance like that. Her mom thought American dancing looked silly.

"You like my new poster of these guys?" Emily shouted above the music.

Aruna looked at the wall where Emily pointed and saw a poster of three boys with hair falling in their faces.

"They are *so* cute," Amber sighed loudly. "I would die to go out with them."

Aruna liked the way they looked too. But she knew she would not go out with boys like that. Maybe she could go out with an Indian boy. But of course it was wrong to date, her mom said. Anyway, she didn't think any boy would want to go out with her. She figured she'd get married like her mother and father did — an arranged marriage. She didn't think she'd mind, because otherwise no one would marry her at all.

After a while Amber said she was going home — her mom was taking her shopping. So Aruna said she'd go home too. No one protested. As they were leaving, Emily promised to call Amber that evening about the movie they were going to see the next day. They didn't invite Aruna.

On her way home, Aruna took her rock out of her pocket and examined it. Then she threw it as far away as she could.

When she got home, she was still thinking about the models in the magazine. She went up to the bathroom and looked at herself in the mirror. Her face was round and her skin was brown. Her black eyes looked back at her from behind pink oval glasses. She had straight hair that hung down to the middle of her back, but she always wished it was curly. Some of the finalists in the modeling contest had tan skin — but none as dark as Aruna's. And they all had very small noses. Aruna's nose was plump and large. She turned away from the mirror. She was definitely ugly.

Chapter 4

*A*runa sighed with satisfaction as she sat at the kitchen table. Mom, wearing a red and white checked apron, was just taking an apple pie she had baked out of the oven, and the kitchen was filled with the sweet cinnamon scent of it. Through the doorway to the dining room Aruna could see a large patchwork quilt, with intricate multicolored star panels, displayed on the wall. Under the kitchen table she rubbed her leg against the long silky hair of Idaho, a part-collie mutt. Aruna smiled. She was so glad she lived in the perfect American house!

"Want ice cream with your pie, Aruna?" Darcy's words broke into Aruna's daydream.

"Sure," Aruna said, and accepted the plate full of pie and vanilla ice cream that Darcy handed her. Oh, well. So it was her new friend *Darcy's* house that was the perfect American house. At least she had a best friend, finally.

She had met Darcy in the school library one day, when her class was looking for books to do book reports on. Someone had tapped her on the shoulder, and she turned around to see a girl from her class with short brownish-blond hair and very green eyes holding out a book to her. Aruna knew her name was Darcy, but they had never really talked before.

"How 'bout this book?" Darcy whispered. Aruna looked at the cover of the book — it was about Mahatma Gandhi and the Indian independence movement — and shook her head. Aruna *never* did book reports about India. She hated whenever they studied anything about India in class. All the other kids would turn around and stare at her. As soon as the teacher even mentioned the word "India," she'd hear the dreaded sound of twenty kids turning and craning their necks at her, like she was a specimen on display. She certainly wasn't going to do a book report on India and remind everyone even more about how different she was.

After Aruna refused the book, Darcy decided to read it herself. Then she asked Aruna to play kickball with a bunch of other kids at recess, and that's how they became friends.

Darcy was a really nice girl — not like Amber and Emily. She didn't talk about her hair or clothes all the time. She liked to wear old flannel shirts over her jeans. She liked to explore in the woods near their school, just like Aruna did. And she could even say Aruna's name almost perfectly. She didn't say "A-ROO-nuh" like everyone else did. She understood that there was no strong accent on any syllable, except to draw out the last one — "A-runaa."

Unfortunately, Darcy lived in a different neighborhood so they hardly saw each other outside of school. But today, Darcy had invited her over for the afternoon! They were going to hunt for insects and rocks in the field next to Darcy's house. Darcy was into entomology.

As Aruna sat across from Darcy at the kitchen table, giggling and eating, she tried to pretend that Darcy was really her sister, and that Darcy's mom was *her* mom.

"Mmm, this pie is great, Mrs. Stewart," Aruna said as she shoveled in spoonfuls of the sweet sticky pie and cold ice cream.

"Thank you." Mrs. Stewart sat down at the table with the girls and smoothed back her short curly brown hair. "It's my mother's recipe. She always won prizes for it at the county fair."

The county fair! How perfect, Aruna thought. She could picture Mrs. Stewart's mom, a smiling white-haired woman in a neat print dress, standing outdoors at a long table laden with pies — lattice-topped blackberry, cherry, strawberry — but *her* apple pie had the big blue ribbon next to it. In the background Aruna pictured a bandstand, and nearby maybe a Ferris wheel.

Aruna's grandmother in India could never win a contest like that — she didn't own an oven and had never even tasted a pie, probably, in her life!

"Darcy tells me you're from India," Mrs. Stewart was saying.

Aruna scooped up another spoonful of pie. "Yeah," she said with her mouth full.

"I hear it's a fascinating country," Mrs. Stewart went on. "So mysterious and exotic."

Aruna didn't want to talk about India right now. She wished people didn't always start talking to her about India as soon as they saw her brown face. She wished she looked like Darcy, with freckles and green eyes.

"I don't remember India that well," Aruna said between bites. "But I don't think it's mysterious. It's just a different way to live." She remembered her old, fat grandmother and her uncles who slurped when they ate. Nothing mysterious about that.

"You must miss your family there," Mrs. Stewart said as she cleared away the plates.

Aruna didn't miss them at all — she almost wouldn't have remembered them except that she saw photos they sent over, and Mom reminded her of who everyone was. But she didn't have time to explain all this to Mrs. Stewart — Darcy was already at the front door calling her, and she got up to go.

"Thanks for the pie!" she yelled as she ran out the door with Darcy.

It was a beautiful crisp fall day. The sky was a clear bright blue, and the trees blazed red and yellow. Darcy's house was in an older part of town, where tall trees over-hung the street, and where the houses had porches and even cute white picket fences.

They ran through the tall field grass, studded with nodding goldenrod and pretty Queen Anne's lace, towards a little stream Darcy knew about. Suddenly Darcy stopped and said, "Watch out!" Aruna looked down at her feet and there was the little stream — completely invisible until you were almost in it!

All afternoon they watched the waterbugs skate on the stream, and tried to figure out the exact colors of the damselflies that darted above the water. Aruna peered into the stream at all the pretty pebbles — white and pink and glittering gold and glossy black. She put her hands into the cool water to scoop up some fine gravel and pretended she was panning for gold. Darcy picked up large green beetles and watched them crawl on her hands.

When they were thoroughly tired and their feet were a little too wet for comfort, they trooped home to Darcy's house where Aruna's mom was going to pick her up. Aruna's jacket pockets felt heavy with the weight of the rocks she had collected. She knew they wouldn't look as pretty once they were dry as they did underwater, but she couldn't re-sist picking some up to take home.

As they reached the house Mrs. Stewart met them at the door and said, "Aruna, would you like to stay for supper? I think this is the last nice fall day we'll have, and I thought we may as well cook out."

"Sure!" Aruna exclaimed. More American perfection! She called her mom, and then she and Darcy helped bring out plates and cups and lemonade to the picnic table in the back yard.

Darcy's dad stood in front of the grill flipping hamburgers, wearing an apron that said, "Kiss the Cook." Aruna couldn't imagine her dad wearing an apron like that. She had never even seen her parents kiss each other!

As the setting sun threw an orange glow behind the Stewarts' grill, Aruna sighed and bit into her burger oozing with ketchup, mustard, and relish. A pile of creamy potato salad sat on her plate waiting for her fork. What a perfect day!

Chapter 5

*A*runa's stomach felt like it had butterflies in it, as she sat in the car on the way to Sunday school. Her dad was in the driver's seat wearing a cream-colored silk jubba under his winter coat. Mom sat next to him in a patterned silk sari. Aruna wore her dancing outfit: leggings, a long T-shirt, and a sash around her waist.

This wasn't the first time Aruna had been to Sunday school — she had been there many times already. She took Bharata Natyam dance classes, which was fun, and an Indian culture class. Mom and Dad had a Bhagavad Gita reading and discussion in another classroom.

At first, Aruna hadn't wanted to go to Sunday school. All the girls her age had already taken dance lessons for a while, so Aruna would have to start with the 5 and 6 year olds! She refused to do that, so the first few times at Sunday school, she had just gone with her parents to their Bhagavad Gita reading.

Then Mom had arranged for Aruna to take some private lessons with the dance teacher so she could catch up with her age group. She learned quickly, and in a few months she was able to join the girls of her age. She liked the dance classes, and most of the other girls were pretty friendly.

But today Aruna was nervous and excited about going to Sunday school. Sitting beside her on the back seat was Darcy, who was coming to Sunday school to visit that day! Aruna hoped Darcy would have a good time, and that she would find the Indian classes fun, not weird.

Darcy seemed to be having a great time already. She smiled and pelted Mom and Dad with questions about how a sari is wrapped, why Indian women wear dots on their foreheads, whether Hindu people read the Bible, and any other question about India she could think of.

Mom and Dad happily told her that the forehead dot was a traditional decoration that Hindu women wore, that Hindu people didn't read the Bible -- they had different religious books, and on and on. They *liked* explaining Indian things to Americans. They were always flattered when Americans were interested in India.

But Aruna was bored with all the answers, and embarrassed by all the questions Darcy was asking. She wished she had a normal family, so her friends wouldn't have to ask so many questions! She looked at Darcy, at her very white skin, green eyes, tiny nose, and thin lips. Darcy would look so out of place at Sunday school. And she would probably ask everyone all sorts of questions like she was doing now, and embarrass Aruna.

She sighed and looked out the car window, at the lamp poles hung with green and red Christmas decorations that hadn't been taken down yet, and wondered whether she should ever have asked Darcy to come along.

The car slowed and turned into the school parking lot where the Sunday school was held. Dad cranked up the parking brake, and everyone got out and slammed the car doors shut.

As soon as they swung open the big glass doors to the school, they were greeted by a crowd of Indians milling in the school hallways. Aruna always thought it was funny to see so many women in swaying, bright-colored saris among the gray school lockers, and to hear so many Indian accents echoing off the walls lined with pictures of fresh-faced white kids wearing football uniforms or waving pompoms. Aruna said "hi" to a few other girls in the hall and introduced Darcy to them.

Dance class went fine. Aruna was pleased that Darcy sat quietly in a corner of the gym, where the class was held, and didn't ask questions about why they danced barefoot, or why they said a prayer before and after class. The dance teacher tapped out a beat with a wooden stick, and Darcy watched silently as Aruna and the other kids slapped their feet on the floor and hopped around, moving their hands in unison. Aruna had already learned over a dozen hand positions representing snakes, lions, flowers, or different gods and goddesses.

Sonal Vatsya was also in this class, and Aruna was always secretly pleased to see that she wasn't very good at dancing, even if she *was* a tennis star. She could never keep to the beat.

After dance class, Aruna put her socks and shoes back on and walked with Darcy down the hall to the culture class. They had to dodge through children who were racing around and yelling. Darcy said, "Wow, that dance looks really hard. You're really good!"

"It's not too hard," Aruna said, but she smiled proudly. She was glad Darcy liked the class. She started to feel OK about having invited her.

They slid into chairs in the culture class. The teacher was a tall, smiling woman named Mrs. Bose, and they were continuing their discussion of the different religions of India. All went smoothly until Mrs. Bose asked if anyone had any questions. Aruna saw Darcy's white arm waving in the air.

"Yes?" said Mrs. Bose, nodding at Darcy.

"I was wondering . . . what holiday do Indian people have at Christmastime? Do they have something like Hanukkah, the way Jewish people do?"

Aruna cringed inside and stared down at the desk. She had heard that question so often! Why did everyone assume all religions had a holiday at Christmastime?

"Very good question," said Mrs. Bose. "Who has an answer?"

Several brown arms waved in the air, and kids shouted answers. "Some Indians are Christian, so they celebrate Christmas," a boy with large black-framed glasses said.

"Excellent point," Mrs. Bose said.

"Hindus don't have a big holiday at Christmastime," Sonal said. "But at our house we have a Christmas tree anyway because we like to get presents."

Someone else said, "Diwali is like Christmas, because we decorate the house with lights."

"That's true," Mrs. Bose agreed, "but what month is Diwali in?"

"October or November!" Aruna heard herself chime in. "It's not like Christmas at all! There's no tree to decorate, and we don't get tons of presents. Why do we have to compare all holidays to Christmas? In our house we don't celebrate Christmas. We all go out to see a movie on that day."

"Good point, Aruna," Mrs. Bose agreed. "You are right — every religion has its own holidays at different times of the year."

Finally, Sunday school was over. They drove Darcy back to her house. On the way Darcy said, "That was fun! You're so lucky to be Indian, Aruna, and to go to Indian Sunday school. My Sunday school is so boring. See you later!" Darcy slammed the car door shut and ran into her house.

Aruna didn't feel lucky to be going to Indian Sun-

day school. She wished she could go to a boring, normal
Sunday school. But at least Darcy had enjoyed herself —
and fortunately, she wouldn't be going with them the next
Sunday.

Chapter 6

*A*runa was trying to be extra good today. She had to ask her mom for permission to do something, and she wasn't sure Mom would say "yes." When she came home after school she closed the front door quietly instead of slamming it. She took her sneakers off and slid them neatly into the shoe rack. Then she went upstairs and put her books in her room, instead of tossing them onto the sofa in the family room.

There were lots of things Aruna wasn't allowed to do, like watch any TV shows where they talked about sex or said bad words or shot people, or ride in a car driven by a teenager, or sleep over at someone else's house unless her parents knew the family really well. Kids didn't do things like that in India, so Aruna couldn't do them either, which didn't seem logical since they didn't live in India anymore.

Aruna went into the kitchen, where Mom was making dinner, and asked if she could help. Her mom loved it when Aruna helped her cook.

"You want to cut the cucumbers for pachadi?" Mom asked.

Aruna peeled the cucumbers Mom gave her, and sat at the table to cut them. She tried to make sure each piece was small and evenly-shaped.

"So what did you do today?" Mom asked. She was rinsing dal at the sink.

Aruna thought carefully before she answered. She wanted to say something that would make Mom happy. Finally she remembered something and said, "I got an A on my math test."

"Very good! Tell Daddy when he comes home," Mom said. She measured some salt into her palm and tossed it into the pot.

"OK," said Aruna. She positioned the next cucumber and started to slice it carefully. Should she ask her mom now? she wondered. She might as well.

"Mom, Darcy told me about this really neat summer camp she's going to this summer, where they have painting lessons, and horseback riding, and hiking, and a lake to swim in, and all sorts of stuff, and she asked if I could go to the camp with her. She says it's really safe, and the camp counselors are really nice, and nothing bad ever happens, so can I go?" Aruna sliced the cucumber slowly, waiting to hear what Mom would say.

Mom was bending down rummaging for a pot lid in a cabinet. She found it, then straightened up and said,

"We were going to tell you soon, Aruna. This summer we are going to India. We didn't want to tell you until the tickets were confirmed. The travel agent just called before you came in and said everything is settled. So you will have to tell Darcy you can't go, because you are going to see your relatives this summer."

Aruna dropped her knife on the table and stared at her mother. How could her parents do this to her? First they moved her away from all her friends. Then when she found a friend who asked her to go to summer camp with her, they were going to drag her off to India!

"How come you didn't ask me if I wanted to go to India?" she shouted. "How come I never get to decide anything around here? You treat me like I'm a little baby who doesn't care what it does! I'm a person and I have a life too, and I don't want to go to India!"

Mom turned back to the stove and put the lid on the pot. "You have a life, yes. But who gave you that life? We are your parents, and we are doing what is best for you. We want you to know your relatives in India. We should have taken you before. But you know Daddy was just an assistant professor at first, and then we were sending money to India for your aunties who were still in college. Then we bought this house, so you would have a nice yard to play in. So this summer, finally, we are going to India. And I am going to see my mother. I have not been home in almost seven years."

Aruna knew her mom missed India. But she was

still angry.

"If India is so great, how come you left? If you wanted me to know my relatives, how come you brought me here? I don't want to go to India! I want to go to summer camp!" Aruna felt a lump in her throat, and she knew she was about to start crying, even though she didn't want to. Crying was babyish, and she was trying to prove she was a grown girl with opinions of her own. But what was the use? She never won any arguments with her mother. She put her head on her arms down on the table and burst into tears of frustration and anger.

"Cry all you want, you are going to India," Mom said. "You want to know why we brought you here? Everybody says America has the best educational and job opportunities. And we thought you would appreciate being here. Instead, you have just become selfish and loud, like an American. When I was growing up, I would never ever shout at my mother like that. The problem with you is you don't respect your elders."

Aruna had heard this lecture about how disrespectful she was many times. Mom said she used to be afraid if her father even *spoke* to her. Aruna could hear Mom bustling around the kitchen as she sniffled with her head in her arms. It was clear she wasn't going to get any sympathy, so she scraped back her chair noisily (she didn't care about being good anymore), climbed heavily up the stairs to her room, and slammed the door as hard as she could. She picked her way to her bed amid two days of clothes strewn on the floor, and threw herself down on it.

She lay on her back with her arms crossed. She never got to do *anything* she wanted. Even her bedroom furniture — she looked around at it — wasn't her own choice. She'd wanted a roll-top desk, with lots of pigeon-holes where she could stash secret things. But Mom *made* her pick out a *matching* set of *ugly* furniture. Aruna glared at the ceiling. They'd *made* her move and leave all her friends behind. And now this trip to India on top of every-thing. Aruna felt like she had no control over her life. She just had to do whatever her parents said.

She rolled onto her side and rested her head on her arm. What did she remember about India? She'd just started kindergarten when they'd left. She remembered living with her dad's family, her ajji and thatha, her two aunties, Sharmila and Vandana, who were still in school, and in another house nearby, her uncle and auntie and cousins. There was always something going on in the house, always someone to hug her and play with her. They all thought she was very cute and smart. She could speak Kannada fluently then, her mother said, and was starting to learn English in school.

But now what would her relatives think of her? She wasn't a little girl anymore. She was a skinny, big-nosed, stringy-haired girl who could speak only English fluently.

She was starting to feel cold, so she climbed under the covers. She must have dozed off. The next thing she heard was her door opening slowly.

"Raja, come and eat," she heard her mom say softly. She opened her eyes and turned over to face her mom. Why was she in bed? Then she remembered — she was angry. But she was also hungry. She must have slept till dinnertime.

"Come on, eat your dinner and you'll feel better," Mom coaxed, helping her out of bed.

As they walked downstairs Mom said, "Aruna, I didn't tell you one big reason we are going to India. They have found a boy for Sharmila! Her marriage is fixed for July, and we will attend the wedding. Won't that be fun?"

Aruna smiled and agreed, still too drowsy to think very clearly. She remembered liking Sharmila because her auntie taught her how to draw and let her use her colored pencils. How odd, though, for Sharmila to be getting married! That was for grown-ups. Aruna remembered Sharmila as a big girl who rode her bike to school in her blue school uniform dress, her long braids hanging down her back.

India would be so different when she went back. She followed her mother into the kitchen and sat down to dinner, still dazed from sleep and the news of the trip.

Chapter 7

"**A**runa, can't you pack some nice clothes?" Mom lifted out the neat stack of shorts Aruna had placed in the suitcase. "Your ajji will not want to see you in these shorts all the time. Hurry up, get some proper clothes so we can finish packing!" Mom turned to fold another frilly little girl's dress for one of Aruna's cousins.

Aruna slouched out of her parents' bedroom and back to her own room. What was there to wear in summer if not shorts? She pawed through the clothes in her closet and extracted a few pairs of below-the-knee leggings, and some baggy jeans. She opened her dresser drawer and pulled out several oversized T-shirts.

Aruna flung herself on her bed to think things over, with her clothes draped over her arm. When she'd told Darcy she couldn't go to summer camp because she was going to India instead, Darcy's eyes got wide and she said, "You are so lucky!" Aruna wasn't so sure — she had been really looking forward to riding a horse at camp. But she did show Darcy pictures of all her relatives, and even drew a family tree of her dad's family — whose house they would stay in. It looked like this:

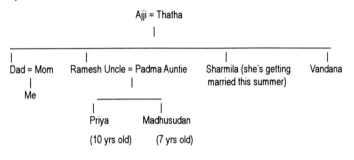

" 'Ajji' is the word for grandmother," Aruna had explained, "and 'Thatha' is grandfather. My dad's the oldest in his family, and his two sisters, Sharmila and Vandana, are a lot younger than him. Sharmila is 22 and Vandana is 21. I don't even have to call them 'auntie' if I don't want to."

"That is so neat!" Darcy had sighed as she looked at the photographs. She had asked Aruna to write to her from India, and promised to write to Aruna from camp.

A warm summer breeze wafted through the window as Aruna lay on the bed still clutching the clothes she had to pack. In her mind she went through all the things she had to remember on this trip.

She wasn't supposed to talk loudly or contradict an adult. When she sat on the floor she wasn't supposed to stretch her legs out so her soles pointed to someone, or to a picture of a god or goddess. No shoes or sandals should be worn in the house, especially not in the kitchen or the "God's room."

When she ate with her fingers, she should take care that no food soiled her hand beyond the second knuckles on her fingers. When she accepted something from some-one else, especially prasada, she had to use her right hand or both hands, and never the left hand only. It was bad luck to step over someone who was lying on the floor.

When she spoke in her halting Kannada, there were certain word endings she had to add to show respect for older people, but she shouldn't add those when she talked to children, otherwise people would laugh at her. Fortu-nately, most of Aruna's relatives knew English. She hoped she could remember all these rules.

"Aruna!" She heard annoyance in her mom's voice. "I'm going to close the suitcases without your clothes. Come on!"

Aruna sprang off the bed and ran into her mom's bedroom. She rolled the clothes into a ball along the way, and tossed them from the doorway into the suitcase across the room. Two points!

"Fold them neatly, raja," Mom said. She was tuck-ing little plastic razors in the corners of another suitcase on the bed. All the uncles really liked American disposable razors.

As Aruna painstakingly folded her clothes, Mom in-spected them. "Aruna, raja, why don't we go buy you some nice skirts or dresses for the trip?" Mom wheedled. Mom was always trying to get Aruna to wear lacy or ruffled clothes. "You don't want your relatives to think we don't buy you proper clothes. Look at this!" She held up a faded T-shirt. "I can hardly see the design on this thing, it is so old. And so baggy. You will look like a beggar."

Aruna took the T-shirt back and folded it again. "I don't like those fancy dresses you want me to wear."

Mom had spent weeks shopping for this trip. They were taking packs of disposable pens, and plastic barrettes and elastic hair ties for the girl cousins. The aunts were getting delicate machine-made jewelry from the store Mom worked in — most jewelry in India was handmade. Mom had also stocked up on perfumes and lip balms. Some of the aunts were getting decorated ceramic cooking pots. Clothes were a problem: you had to make sure they were made in the U.S. Who wanted shirts and dresses from America that were actually made in China or, even worse, India?

Aruna folded her clothes and pressed them into her overflowing suitcase.

"We'll get you some new clothes to wear at the wedding," Mom said. She was so excited about buying Aruna Indian clothes. "I put a necklace on the dresser. See if you want to wear it at the wedding."

Aruna got up from the floor and bent over the jewelry on the dresser. Her mom had chosen a beautiful necklace. Two rows of perfect cream-colored pearls, and the pendant was a heart-shaped medallion of gold studded with more pearls and red stones. "You're going to let me wear this at the wedding?" Aruna gasped.

"Of course. When you get older you can wear my saris too."

Aruna felt proud that her mom trusted her to wear her best jewelry. She undid the clasp on the necklace, fastened it around her neck, and turned to her mom. "How do I look?"

Her mom looked up from the suitcase. "The necklace looks very pretty. You would look better if you weren't wearing that faded old T-shirt."

Aruna turned back to the mirror. The necklace *was* pretty. But it didn't sit as nicely on her neck as on her mom's. She was too skinny and dark to be pretty, she knew. And her hair was too thin. A pretty Indian woman had a really thick, long braid.

She took the necklace off and laid it carefully back on the dresser. Then she sat on the bed to look at all the presents in the suitcase.

"Do you remember the house in India?" Mom asked. She opened a drawer and lifted out a pile of white cotton petticoats.

"Sure," said Aruna. It was her dad's parents' house they had lived in. "The sparrows used to fly right into the house! And there was a little dark room with a bag of almonds. I wanted to eat them but I couldn't break the shells."

"That was the storeroom," said Mom. "It had a lot

more than just almonds in it. That's where your ajji kept the flour, and raisins, and rice, and dal, and other dry goods."

Aruna rubbed her palm on the smooth, soft cotton of the petticoats Mom put in the suitcase. "My teacher Mrs. Garner was telling us other things about India that I don't remember. There was a picture in our book that showed a man in a turban plowing a field with an ox. I don't remember that."

"That's because we lived in the city," Mom said. "If you go to the villages you will see plenty of farms."

"And Mrs. Garner also said that in India, women burn themselves to death if their husbands die. Is that true?" Aruna demanded. She was sure Mrs. Garner was mistaken about such a horrifying thing.

"Some people used to do that long ago. But it is illegal now. Only a few women did that among the warrior caste. I don't know why Mrs. Garner is telling you all those old, awful things. Americans must think Indians are very backward."

"Did our family do that?" Aruna asked.

"No, we are Brahmins. We did not fight in wars. Long ago we were temple priests I suppose, and at the time of my great-grandfathers they were Sanskrit scholars."

Aruna was entranced. "Sanskrit scholars! That sounds interesting." What if she could read Sanskrit? Then she would be able to read fascinating stories like the ones Dad told about all the Hindu gods and goddesses. "I wish

I could have lived then."

"Only the men were Sanskrit scholars," said Mom. "The women were not given any education, but one of my great-grandmothers learned Sanskrit anyway from her husband. Help me press this down."

Aruna leaned on the suitcase lid while Mom snapped the latches shut.

"Aren't you glad you didn't live when the girls didn't go to school?" Aruna asked Mom.

"I don't know about school, but I'm glad I didn't live then, because they had child marriages," Mom said. She swung the suitcase off the bed and set it on the floor. "They would get a girl engaged when she was very young — sometimes even a baby. Then when she was 13 or 14 she had to marry this man she had never seen. Sometimes he was much older than she was. And then if he died, she was not allowed to marry again, no matter how young she was. She had to remove all her jewelry, wear a plain sari, shave her head, and not socialize with people. Even today some people treat widows this way, but our family is more modern than that." She knelt down and dragged out another suitcase from under the bed.

"I'm glad I didn't have to go through all that," Mom declared as she stood up. "At least I finished college before getting engaged. And at least I was allowed to see your daddy once before the engagement, and to meet him every day afterwards. If I had not liked him, no one would have forced me to marry him." Mom picked up a pile of white undershirts. "OK, let's pack Daddy's things now."

Aruna handed Mom a stack of Dad's socks. Warm yellow sunshine splashed through the window onto the bed. She liked sitting here with her mother, chatting about their relatives and their family history. She hoped she would feel just as comfortable *being* with her relatives.

Chapter 8

*A*runa's heart pounded. She and her parents stood in the waiting room at the Bangalore airport, looking around for their relatives. Would she recognize her relatives when she saw them? She gazed out at the sea of brown faces and saw no one she knew. Skinny Indian men in khaki uniforms hurried around helping people with their luggage. Aruna was hot. The airport was not air-conditioned, and the few fans on the high ceiling didn't seem to do much.

Aruna's head felt woozy from the flying, and from not getting enough sleep. It took 24 hours to reach India from the Cleveland, Ohio airport. After they landed they had to wait a few hours in the airport to clear customs. That was when men in uniforms opened everyone's suitcases to make sure people weren't smuggling things into India that weren't allowed.

Suddenly several people were at their side, and Aruna recognized her grandmother! Aruna's mom dropped her bags and grasped Ajji's hands in her own. Aruna saw tears in her mom's eyes.

Ramesh Uncle smoothed Aruna's hair. "How was your trip, young lady?" he asked.

"Fine." Aruna smiled sheepishly. She was afraid she would say the wrong thing, even though everyone seemed so nice.

Ramesh Uncle and Dad slapped each other on the back and laughed. They were brothers. They collected the luggage and went outside to the parking lot and piled into Ramesh Uncle's car. Aruna sat on a tiny wedge of the back seat between Ajji and her mom.

"Do you remember us?" Ajji asked in Kannada.

"I remember," Aruna said softly.

"Oh, she can still speak Kannada!" exclaimed Padma Auntie.

"She can understand perfectly. She just doesn't like to speak," said Mom.

Aruna's face grew hot with embarrassment. It wasn't that she didn't *like* to speak. She was just afraid of getting laughed at. But she couldn't explain that because she didn't want them to think she was a contradictory, rude American kid.

"That's OK," said Ajji. "Let her speak however much she wants to."

Aruna was grateful for her grandmother's words, but didn't know how to thank her.

The car bumped and rumbled along the road.

"Look, Aruna, the soil is red," Dad said, pointing out the window. He had told her that Bangalore dirt was reddish because of a high iron content — and she saw it was indeed a dull orange color.

The road was lined with scrubby bushes, and the sky was pale. Sometimes they passed a few dark gray water buffaloes with their keeper. The buffaloes swayed and clanked their bells down the side of the road. Aruna breathed the scent of the Indian air and immediately felt more comfortable — she remembered that smell! It was a combination of car exhaust and cow dung and the soft jasmine scent from the white flowers in her aunt's hair.

They were on a main city road now. Aruna was thrown against her mother as they honked their way around a traffic circle crowded with buses, autorikshas, cars, motorcycles, bicycles, and people. Ramesh Uncle pointed out the new buildings. "That is a new movie theater. It can seat 1,000 people. Over there is a 5-star hotel."

Finally the car stopped in front of a house. Aruna recognized it — the house she had lived in! A servant opened the tall gate, and the car rolled in and stopped just inside the wall surrounding the yard. Everyone piled out. Aruna saw Thatha walking towards them, leaning on a cane. Mom pinched the cheeks of a little boy — was it Madhusudan? He was only a baby when Aruna had last seen him. And her other Ajji, Dad's mom, pinched Aruna's cheek. There were people everywhere, patting her head, and offering to carry things from the car. Ramesh Uncle drove the car into the garage, and everyone else went into the house. Aruna followed, tired and hungry from the trip.

◇   ◇   ◇

Aruna tore off a piece of chapati with the fingers of one hand only, as her mother had taught her, and used it to scoop up a little aviyal. She looked in disbelief at the amount of food on her plate: besides 2 chapatis and a large puddle of aviyal, she had a mountain of white rice topped with sambar, and a generous mound of squash palya. Beside her plate was a steel cup of water and another of rasam broth. Her grandmother had just kept serving her until Mom, sitting beside her on a straw mat on the floor, said "That's enough." Then Mom whispered to Aruna with annoyance, "Put your hand over your plate when you don't want any more. Otherwise she will go on serving you."

They had pushed the dining table aside and were sitting on the floor this first evening because there were so many people at dinner who came to see Aruna's family. Arranged along the three walls of the dining room were not only her dad's family, but her mom's mother and sister, and her dad's aunt — Aruna's great-aunt — a fat, wrinkled woman. Even though she was so old she sat on her straw mat with perfect ease, her sari gathered around herself neatly so it didn't fall in her food.

Aruna, on the other hand, was quite uncomfortable on the floor. Her feet were starting to fall asleep from sitting cross-legged so long. The food was too peppery but besides that it didn't have much taste. Aruna wished she could be eating a piece of pizza.

As she tried to get some of the mushy white rice down, she realized to her dismay that the relatives were talking about her!

"So this is your daughter," the great-aunt said loudly to Aruna's mother.

"Here she is," Mom replied.

The woman formed little balls out of her rice and sambar and tossed them into her mouth as she looked Aruna over.

Finally the great-aunt asked Aruna, "Do you know Kannada?"

"I know it," Aruna said softly.

The aunt inspected her some more. Aruna tried hard to eat neatly and not get food all over her palms.

"She looks like a good Indian girl, even though she is from America," the great-aunt pronounced finally.

"Yes, she is very quiet," said her dad's mom.

Aruna was glad she had braided her hair and put a dot on her forehead before dinner.

"She is a little skinny and dark, don't you think?" said the great-aunt. She slurped up the last of her food.

"Nothing can be done about that," said Ajji. "Whatever God gives us, we must take."

Aruna squirmed uncomfortably. This aunt apparently thought it was OK to insult her! Should she say something? She looked up at her mom, who was eating placidly. She looked at everyone else: her dad, Ramesh Uncle, her aunts and cousins. No one seemed to have heard or paid attention to the great-aunt — they just kept eating and drinking.

Then Mom leaned over and whispered in English, "Don't pay any attention, Aruna. She just likes to make comments about everyone."

Aruna shrugged. What did she care what the old woman thought? But it was even harder now to swallow her food with the lump in her throat.

Chapter 9

Aruna tried to stifle a yawn as her cousin Priya talked. She hadn't gotten a good night's sleep in the first few days she had been in India because she was still not used to sleeping on the floor. Now they were bumping along in an autoriksha on their way to go shopping. The heat and the motion made Aruna even more sleepy.

Priya was a nice girl. Even though she was only 10 — over a year younger than Aruna — she was the same height and plumper. Her skin was lighter than Aruna's, and her braids were shiny and thick. Mom kept saying how pretty she was. Aruna didn't think she was all *that* pretty. If Priya went to Aruna's school, the kids might even call her pudgy. But Indians didn't like people to be too skinny.

Priya wanted to be with Aruna all the time. Like now, they were on their way to MG Road (that stood for Mahatma Gandhi Road) to buy Aruna some new clothes for the wedding. Priya insisted on riding in the same autoriksha as Aruna. As they rattled along in the sputtering three-wheeled vehicle, Priya held her hand and talked to her the entire trip. Aruna could hardly hear, the auto was so loud. She just nodded politely at intervals.

And Priya wasn't the only person who liked Aruna. All her relatives seemed really glad to see her. Every morning, as soon as Aruna woke up, Ajji brought her a cup of warm sweetened milk. Yesterday Padma Auntie had gotten up extra early to cook one of Aruna's favorite foods: masala dosa. Vandana and Sharmila made a point of introducing Aruna to any of their friends who dropped by. Aruna couldn't believe she had ever been worried that her relatives wouldn't like her! She felt almost embarrassed by all the attention she was getting.

Still, the first few days in India had been hard. When Aruna stepped into the damp bathroom to use the toilet, she saw huge brown cockroaches scurry into the walls, their long antennae waving. And using the toilet itself was so different. There was no toilet paper in the bathroom — in India people used water. There was a bucket and dipper under a water tap beside the toilet.

Aruna had to place her feet on the ceramic footrests and squat down over the porcelain toilet in the floor. It was hard to balance herself, especially when she used the dipper to wash herself. When she pulled up her pants she was still a little damp.

As she lay on a thin mattress on the floor the first

night, beside the bed her mom and dad were in, she saw a skinny gray lizard clinging to the wall high above her. She stared at it for a long time. She wondered whether it would move or go away.

Just as she was about to fall asleep, she felt something crawl over her neck. "Aah!" she screamed, and flung the covers off. She brushed at her neck, but nothing was there. She couldn't sleep all night because she was afraid a lizard would fall on her, or a roach would crawl on her. Finally, her mom let Aruna get into the bed, and Aruna's dad had to sleep on the floor.

Mom told Aruna that all Indian houses had cockroaches and lizards because the climate was so warm. It was hard to get rid of them even in the fanciest houses. But this didn't make it any easier for Aruna to deal with them.

Aruna's thoughts were interrupted as the auto swerved to the side of the road and stopped abruptly. That's where they were to get off. Padma Auntie paid the auto driver, and they stepped out at a broad main road lined with trees and vast white-fronted stores with signs in English and Kannada. It smelled of bus exhaust. They waited for the other auto that held Mom and Vandana. Sharmila couldn't come along because she had to go to her job at the bank.

A group of laughing young women walked by them, some with short hair, some with long braids and jasmine flowers in their hair. They wore salvar kameez in bright colors, the long tunics embroidered with flowers or designs. Aruna felt silly in her baggy T-shirt and sneakers with no socks. Everyone must know she was not from India! Even Priya fit in. She wore a new white and pink dress from America with a ruffle at the bottom, and chappals. Now Aruna wished she had listened to her mother and bought some more skirts or dresses. People in India seemed to dress fancy just to go shopping.

A small, squinting beggar woman in a faded sari tottered up to them. She held out her hand and pleaded for money. Padma Auntie said, "Go away! You are always here."

Aruna stared at the bony woman with tangled hair, creased skin, and bare, dusty feet. She wanted to look away, but couldn't take her eyes off the beggar woman. The woman's voice kept whining, "Ma, ma," as she held out her dark, dirty claw-like hands.

Just then the other auto showed up, and Padma Auntie put a hand on Aruna's back. "Come on," Auntie said.

Aruna kept staring at the beggar. Then she whispered to Padma Auntie, "Let me give her something." Auntie gazed at Aruna for a second, shook her head, snapped open her purse, and extracted some paisa. "Here," she said, and dropped the coins into the woman's hand. The woman put her palms together in front of her face, then shuffled off.

"You will get used to the beggars," Padma Auntie

assured Aruna as they hurried into a department store with everyone else. "We cannot give money to everyone who asks."

The store was large, light-filled, and air-conditioned — not nearly as big as an American department store, but much bigger than the tiny, dark storefronts Aruna had seen from the auto near their house.

Padma Auntie rummaged briskly through the racks of clothing, and pulled out two skirt and blouse outfits. One was red, and one was cream-colored. Both were heavily embroidered with gold thread. "Do you like either of these?" Padma Auntie asked. The silk material shone softly as Padma Auntie held them up for Aruna's inspection.

Aruna thought they were both very nice looking. "Oh, yeah! I like them both." When she heard her own American drawl, it sounded so funny after the Indian voices she'd been hearing.

Vandana had found a few more to show Aruna. They were all pretty. Aruna couldn't decide. She took all the outfits into the dressing room to try them on, and decided the red one, and a black and lavender one selected by Vandana, fit the best.

"We will get some glass bangles to match at the market near our house," Padma Auntie said as Mom paid for the two outfits.

Aruna couldn't believe Mom had let her buy all that. Mom never let her buy expensive jeans or sneakers in America! They always had to be on sale.

But Mom wasn't done shopping yet. Next they went to a small jewelry store, and Mom propelled Aruna up to the glass-topped counter. In the glass case, laid out on red velvet, Aruna could see glittery necklaces, rings, and bangles.

"I would like to see some gold earrings for my daughter," Mom told the woman behind the counter, and Aruna found herself presented with an array: round daisy earrings with pearls in the center, and little bell-like dangling earrings, and gold hoop earrings. "Do you like any?" Mom asked.

Aruna touched the earrings hesitantly. They were all very pretty. But then her eye was caught by something in the next case. "I like those," she said, and pointed to a pair of silver earrings with dangling ovals of faceted purple amethyst. She loved the rich purple glow of amethyst.

"That is too simple," Mom said, waving away the earrings as the clerk tried to put them on the counter. "Choose something gold. How about this one?" Mom pointed to star-shaped earrings with bright red stones.

Aruna thought all the gold earrings were too fussy. And she happened to look at the price of one. She converted the rupees to dollars in her head, and realized her mother was prepared to spend almost $150 for a pair of earrings! She couldn't believe it. "But Mom, can we afford this?" she whispered.

"Shh, let me worry about the money. Look at this one. Beautiful!" Mom pointed to a pair with dangling birds, the eyes made from tiny red stones and the body inlaid with miniscule pearls. The clerk took the pair out of the case for them.

Aruna couldn't understand why her mother was suddenly not concerned with the cost of things. When Aruna had asked for a geology kit for her birthday, that had been too expensive!

"Mom, I don't want these earrings," she said. "Why can't I have that geology kit? Remember, the one with the tiles for the streak test, and a magnifying glass, and a little hammer, and —"

"If you don't want earrings now, let's look at necklaces," Mom said, and pointed out some necklaces. The clerk put the earrings away and lifted out a few necklaces.

Padma Auntie, who had been leaning over another jewelry case with Priya, now said, "Aruna, you may not want jewelry now, but when you are a grown woman you will be glad to have it."

Aruna didn't think so. She thought she would be more glad to have a geology kit than a whole bunch of this gold jewelry. She liked to look at jewelry but she didn't see the sense of spending that much money on it, especially since her mother already had so much jewelry.

In her mind Aruna saw the poor woman in the street who was begging for a few paisa. Aruna didn't like to spend money on jewelry she didn't even want, when the beggar woman didn't even have a clean sari or food to eat. "Mom, you said I could wear your jewelry. So now all I want are those amethyst earrings," she insisted.

But Mom was just as insistent. If Aruna wasn't going to choose something, Mom would choose for her. One way or another, Aruna would have some gold jewelry. Aruna didn't think she could convince Mom to give $150 to the street beggar, so finally she walked out of the store with the bird earrings, the silver amethyst earrings, and a pair of heavy gold bangles.

Aruna felt a little defeated. But Priya, holding her hand as they walked along, said several times, "You are so lucky, Aruna. What cute birds! I want my mother to buy some just like that for me."

When they got home, Aruna was also the owner of a pair of chappals, and some comic books about Hindu religious stories. As soon as everyone had cleared out of the front room, Aruna untied her sneakers and slipped on the bright red Indian chappals. They felt funny because there was a loop of leather around her big toe, and a strap across the top of her foot, but nothing that went around her heel.

She practiced walking up and down the small front living room. She looked down at her feet. They looked Indian! Aruna realized she liked that. She liked looking Indian in India. She took off the chappals and settled into a chair to read her comic books.

Chapter 10

She opened the first comic book — the story of the Princess Savitri. Before Savitri was born, her parents had no children. Her father the King prayed and fasted for 18 years, asking the gods for a son. Finally a goddess appeared before him and promised that he would have a daughter. Savitri was born soon after.

Aruna saw a drawing of the beautiful Princess Savitri, with large, long-lashed eyes and light skin. Savitri was a very devoted daughter, as well as being talented at music, philosophy, astronomy, and other subjects.

> One day Princess Savitri's father told Savitri it was time for her to be married. Because she was so accomplished and beautiful, none of the princes nearby dared to propose marriage to her. So the King told Savitri to choose her own husband.
> Savitri set out in a chariot, with many people

in attendance, to find a husband. But instead of visiting other palaces, she entered the forest to visit the holy men there.

Savitri went from one hermitage to another, paying her respects to the holy men. Finally, after traveling far into the forest, Savitri saw a young man chopping wood.

As she gazed at him, their eyes met. He was wearing tattered clothing made of bark, but from his eyes she could tell he was a noble and virtuous man.

Savitri asked people at a nearby hermitage who he was, and found out he was Prince Satyavan. He lived in the forest because his father, who was blind, had been driven out of his kingdom and into the forest.

Savitri knew she wanted Satyavan for her husband. She rode back to her own palace to tell her father whom she had chosen.

But when she got back home and told her father she wanted to marry Prince Satyavan, the holy sage Narada, who was visiting, warned Savitri not to marry Satyavan. "Satyavan is indeed a brilliant and generous man," said Narada. "But he is destined to die one year from today."

Nevertheless, Savitri insisted that she would not change her mind. She told her father she had chosen Satyavan in her heart, and could not go back on her decision.

After they were married, Savitri stopped wearing her fancy clothes and jewelry. She dressed in a plain white sari, and went to live in the forest with Satyavan and his parents. She attended to her mother-in-law and father-in-law, smiling cheerfully. But she kept remembering that soon her husband would die.

The week before Satyavan was to die, Savitri fasted and prayed for three days and three nights. The next day, even though she was weak from hunger, Savitri insisted on going with Satyavan as he went out to chop wood. This was the day he was destined to die!

Savitri sat and watched as Satyavan worked. As he chopped wood, he started to feel ill. Finally he stopped, too weak to go on. He lay down on the ground, and Savitri put his head in her lap.

Just then she saw in front of her a large, green-skinned man wearing a crown and riding a bull. "Who are you?" Savitri cried.

"I am Yama, the God of Death," the green-skinned man said. "I do not normally speak to humans, but you are an extraordinary person. I am here because your husband's time on earth is over." Then he lifted out Satyavan's soul and started carrying it away.

But Savitri would not give up. She followed

Yama as he rode away with Satyavan's soul. Yama tried to persuade Savitri to go back. "You cannot follow me into the realm of the dead. Go back and prepare for your husband's funeral."

But Savitri said, "Wherever my husband goes, I will follow. I have no life without my husband."

Yama was impressed with these words and granted Savitri any wish — except for the life of her husband. Savitri asked that her father-in-law's blindness be cured. Yama granted this wish.

Still Savitri followed the God of Death. She would not turn back. She walked on and on. Yama then told her to ask for another wish — anything but Satyavan's life. Savitri asked for her father-in-law to be restored to his kingdom again. That wish was also granted.

And still Savitri followed Yama. Finally he said he would grant her one more wish — but then she must depart. Savitri asked that 100 sons be born to her and Satyavan. Yama agreed to this and said, "Now you must go back."

But Savitri had outwitted Yama. "God of Death," she said, "the wish you have granted me cannot come true unless you release Satyavan. Please restore him to life. Without my husband I feel I am dead too."

Yama was so impressed with Savitri's devo-

tion and wisdom that he freed Satyavan's soul. Savitri hurried back to where she had left Satyavan's body, and laid his head in her lap again. He woke up as from a deep sleep, and smiled at her.

Aruna closed the comic book. She thought it was very brave of Savitri to follow the God of Death and get her husband back. But did she have to ask for 100 sons? One would have been enough to get Satyavan back, Aruna thought.

Chapter 11

"What, Aruna, sitting here all alone?" Aruna was so absorbed in the story of Savitri that she was startled to find her aunt Vandana standing beside her. "Sharmila is home from her job and has brought some snacks. We are having them on the back steps. Come!" Vandana wore an old tan salvar kameez, small gold studs in her ears, and no other jewelry. She had a very short cap of hair.

Still clutching the comic book, Aruna followed Vandana through the house to the back door, where Sharmila and Priya were already sitting and giggling about something. Sharmila looked quite different from her sister. She wore a bright green salvar kameez with yellow embroidery, and gold bangles, large hoop earrings, a tiny gold stud in her nose, and a gold chain with an ornate pendant. Her long hair was combed smoothly back into a thick braid, except for her short curled bangs. Sharmila was telling Priya a funny story about some man who worked at the bank with her.

On Sharmila's lap was a newspaper cone full of spicy peanuts. Next to Priya was a plate of sour mango slices with tiny piles of salt and hot pepper to dip them into. Aruna picked up a mango slice, gingerly dipped it into the hot pepper, and bit into it. Mmm! Sour, and sweet, and the pepper made her tongue tingle.

"Did you finish the story of Savitri?" Priya asked. She looked at the comic book in Aruna's hand. "Such a lovely story, no?"

"What is lovely about it?" Vandana demanded. She tossed a few peanuts into her mouth. "Savitri is supposed to be the ideal Hindu woman — so devoted to her husband that she follows Yama. And for what? Just to have the pleasure of serving her husband again." Vandana seemed almost angry, even though she tried to smile.

"Vandana, it's only a story," Sharmila said.

"That is true," said Vandana, "and I hope you will not be so selflessly devoted to your husband once you are married."

"I don't see anything wrong with being a devoted wife," Sharmila said, tossing her braid over her shoulder. "But if you are worried I will follow Yama, don't worry, I won't."

There was a silence. Aruna could hear Priya crunching on a mouthful of peanuts. Aruna could eat only one peanut at a time, because they were too spicy for her. Then Vandana spoke again.

"I am just worried about you, Sharmi. You know we hear all sorts of stories about brides who are beaten at their new homes. You must not be a devoted wife in a case like that. You must leave and come straight back here to us."

"Vandana, you are spending too much time at your women's group," Sharmila said. "All you people ever talk about is wife-abuse. I don't know anyone who is abused. Sometimes I think those people at your group are making it all up."

"You don't hear about it because no one would admit they are abused," Vandana said. "They are afraid of gossip. But I know for a fact that one of your college-mates is abused by her husband."

"Oh, who is it?" Sharmila asked with curiosity.

"You know I can't say. We are a confidential group."

"You are a confidential group so you can say whatever you want. Santosh is not that kind of man. And you yourself have met his mother. She is very sweet. Nothing will happen to me there."

"Speaking of Santosh," Priya chimed in, "when is he turning up? I want a ride on his motorcycle."

Santosh was the man Sharmila was to marry. He was very handsome and he visited every day at 4:00 pm, just in time for tea. Priya always tried to get a ride on his motorcycle, and sometimes succeeded.

"Santosh just rang up," Sharmila said. "He can't make it today. He has to meet with some fellow at the office. Too bad for him. We are eating all the snacks without him!" Sharmila laughed and bit into a slice of mango, but the next minute her face looked thoughtful and a little sad.

Vandana and Sharmila chatted for a few minutes about the preparations for Sharmila's wedding, and started talking in Kannada about a lot of friends and relatives who would be attending the wedding.

Aruna's mind wandered as she nibbled her mango slice. She thought about whether *she* would be as devoted a wife as Savitri. She thought not, since she wasn't a devoted daughter, like Savitri. She was sometimes very rude and yelled at her parents, instead of cheerfully doing everything they asked. But even though she wasn't as devoted as Savitri, she thought she would like to be as brave and wise as Savitri.

"So, Aruna, do you have many American friends at your school?" Sharmila's words brought Aruna out of her thoughts. "Or only Indian friends?"

Aruna was surprised at this question. "There aren't very many Indian kids at my school. There's only one other Indian girl in my grade and I don't like her very much."

"Eh, Sharmila, what a silly question!" Vandana said. "Aruna must consider herself American, after all. She left India when she was so young."

"What are you talking about?" demanded Sharmila. "She is an Indian citizen, and she looks Indian. So how can she be an American?"

"Just listen to her speak, Sharmila. She speaks like an American. If you were telephoning her you would say she is American."

"I am not telephoning her, she is right in front of me, and I see that Aruna is Indian."

Aruna looked back and forth at her aunts as they discussed what she was. Finally, Vandana turned to her and said, "What do you say, Aruna? Are you Indian or American?"

Up until that moment Aruna had always thought she was Indian. But Vandana had a point. Even though she *looked* Indian, she *talked* like an American. She liked American food a lot better than most Indian food. And when she thought of "home" she thought of their new house in Ohio — not this house in India, which her dad called "home."

"I don't know!" Aruna heard herself answer to Vandana's question.

"So you mix with all the American girls?" Sharmila asked.

"Not all of them," Aruna said. "My best friend is Darcy. But there are some mean girls too." She was thinking of Amber and Emily. "They talk about their clothes and hair all the time. I think they don't like me because I'm so ugly."

"Girls like that are best avoided," Vandana pronounced. "Stick with the girls who study hard and who are kind."

Sharmila didn't say anything. She was scrutinizing Aruna's face. Finally she said, "Aruna, have you thought about getting your hair cut and styled?"

"Sharmila!" Vandana exploded. "I cannot believe you are suggesting a fashion makeover for such a young girl!"

"Calm down, Vandana. After all, you have short hair yourself. Aruna must keep up with the times. The girls in America are more sophisticated." Sharmila slid closer to Aruna on the step and started patting and fluffing Aruna's hair. "I know a very good beautician who can give you a great style. I am planning to get my hair cut and curled after my wedding. You can go with me then. Priya, go and get me those magazines on the table next to the TV."

Vandana shook her short mop of hair and sighed loudly. "I cut my hair because it is easier to care for this way," she said. "I don't go spending hours curling it, and oiling and braiding it, the way you do, Sharmi."

Sharmila didn't answer, but just took the fashion magazines Priya brought her. "This one we don't need," she said, and handed one of the magazines back to Priya. Aruna saw it was called *Manushi*. "That is Vandana's feminist magazine. No pictures of hair styles in there."

Vandana snatched her magazine out of Priya's hand. "Aruna would do much better to read this than any of that rubbish."

Vandana went back inside. Aruna, Sharmila, and

Priya started examining the hair styles of actresses and models in the magazines. Aruna imagined how Emily and Amber would look at her with awe when she came back to school with long curly hair, or a short bouncy style, or . . .

Chapter 12

Dear Darcy,

How are you? I am fine. India is really fun, so far. All my relatives are so nice, especially my aunties, Sharmila and Vandana. I'm glad we came here. Next week is my aunt Sharmila's wedding.

The house here seems smaller than before! I guess I got bigger. It is one story tall, and the outside is white. The house has no hallways. Every room leads into another room. There are 3 bedrooms, 2 living rooms, 1 dining room, 1 kitchen, and 2 bathrooms. Outside is a big cube of granite, it comes up to my waist, where the clothes are washed. The servant beats the clothes on the rock. My cousin Priya and her little brother Madhusudan and her parents Ramesh Uncle and Padma Auntie live in a smaller house next door. They have 2 bedrooms, 1 living room, 1 dining room, 1 kitchen, and 1 bath-

room. They have a washing machine, but no clothes dryer.

There are no carpets on the floors. It would be too hot. The floors are red and smooth. I don't know what they are made of. In the bathroom there is no shower or bathtub. The floor is made of bumpy granite, with a square depression for where you stand and take a bath. You have to mix hot and cold water in a big bucket and use a dipper to pour the water on yourself. The best part is the sandalwood soap. It smells like perfume!

I sleep in the main house right now, except that Priya wants me to sleep with her. My aunties Sharmila and Vandana moved out of their bedroom so we could use it. They sleep in the big living room. My grandmother sleeps in a little bedroom that is also the storage room. My grandfather sleeps in the front bedroom. He has fat bushy white eyebrows, like a bald eagle. He is kind of scary-looking but nice. He is always trying to get me to eat bananas. We have different kinds of bananas here: short fat ones, red ones, small thin ones (only as long as my dad's finger), and regular ones. They are all good.

I think you would like it here. The only things you would have trouble with are: 1) The food. I really need some grilled cheese. And some cereal. 2) The cockroaches. Before you go into the bath-room you have to turn on the light and wait till all the cockroaches go back into the cracks. Then you can go in. They don't like the light. They are pretty big, maybe 2 inches long. Once when I was standing in a doorway a big one fell on me! Mom brushed it off and when I saw what it was I screamed! They are awful.

But other than that you would like it here. There are lots of mosquitoes at night. We have to burn mosquito coils to keep them away. And we have lizards on the walls sometimes, about 3 inches long and gray. At first I was afraid of them, but now I think they're cute.

And guess what? I'm going to get my hair cut and styled!

Write soon.

Your friend,
Aruna

Aruna folded the air-mail letter carefully and stuck the flaps down. She and Priya were going to walk to the mailbox and drop the letter off, on their way to pick up some sari blouses at the tailor around the corner.

Priya strolled into the bedroom, fanning herself with an Archie comic book. "It's so hot!" She threw herself onto the bed. "You've rubbed off your kumkum, Aruna."

It was hard to remember not to touch her forehead and rub off her kumkum. Aruna slid off the bed and tucked her letter into the front of her skirt. At least she was starting to look more Indian — Priya had loaned her a skirt and blouse, and Mom had bought her a pair of silver ankle chains with tinkly bells. She jingled her way to the little mirror on the steel clothes cabinet and carefully stuck on another tiny black velvet dot.

"Let's go and come back fast!" Priya pushed herself off the bed. "We don't want to miss Santosh. I want him to give me a ride on his motorcycle.

They said goodbye to Mom, Padma Auntie, Ajji, and Sharmila, who were in the big living room talking and making tiny origami boxes to be filled with turmeric and red kumkum powder and given to guests at Sharmila's wedding reception. Priya and Aruna slipped on their chappals and ran out the door onto the dusty road with tall light-green trees arching over it.

Aruna was careful to watch where she stepped, so she wouldn't put her foot into any cow dung. Cows were allowed to wander the streets as they wished. It was fun to feed them banana peels.

"I can't wait for Sharmila's wedding!" Priya exclaimed. "If only Vandana wouldn't be so picky they could have a combined wedding. You know Thatha has been looking for a boy for her too because she has just finished her studies. But she has rejected every boy they showed her. She says she doesn't want to get married — she wants to go for further studies. She's very bright, you know. She helps me study for my exams."

They were at the tailor's. It was a small, dark room

wedged in between other tiny storefronts that sold news-papers, vegetables, bananas, or flowers. Aruna liked to look at the bananas. They were displayed still on their stalks. There were so many bananas poking out from each stalk that they looked like banana porcupines.

Priya picked up the package of sari blouses, and on the way home they stopped at a stall selling sugar cane juice. It had two large rollers into which a skinny boy fed thick sugar cane stalks and lemons. The rollers crushed the sugar cane and the lemons, and the juice poured into glasses filled with crushed ice. Priya paid for two glasses, and Aruna took a gulp of the icy liquid. It was like lemonade! They stood and drank their juice, and gave the glasses back to the boy so he could wash them and reuse them.

As they neared home, they saw the front gate was open. "Santosh is there already!" Priya shouted. She took off running, her long braids flying behind her. Aruna followed. "Santosh! Santosh! A ride, please!" Priya shouted as she flew into the yard.

When Aruna ran through the gate, she stopped short. Santosh's motorcycle was parked in front of the door, and Santosh stood on the doorstep listening to Thatha, who spoke in a low voice. They both looked very serious and worried. Santosh did not turn to answer Priya at all. Thatha said quietly, "Priya, please go home. Santosh is not free now."

Priya beckoned to Aruna and whispered, "Something has happened. Let's go to my house and see if my mother is there. Maybe she'll tell us what is the matter."

They crept quietly around the side of the house and through the back gate into Priya's yard. The maid, Lakshmi, sat on the back doorstep shelling peas. She wore an old faded sari. But her hair was combed smoothly into an oiled braid, and she smiled widely at Aruna. She was very curious about Aruna and her family who had come from "foreign," and she liked to stare at Aruna.

"What's up, Lakshmi," Priya said in Kannada as she bounded in the door. "Is my mother here?"

"No, they're all at the other house," Lakshmi replied, still staring and smiling at Aruna, all the while deftly removing peas from their pods.

Priya left the sari blouses on the dining table, grabbed a bunch of grapes from a bowl on the table, handed a portion to Aruna, and ran out the house and to the open back door of the other house. There she crouched, motioned for Aruna to do the same, and put her finger to her lips. "If we remain here quietly we may hear what is going on. Otherwise they may not ever tell us." From the back doorway they could see through the back work area, through the main living room doorway, through the front living room doorway, all the way to the front door.

They leaned against the door frame, listening intently. They heard low, pleading women's voices, and once in a while a wailed "O Rama!" Aruna was scared. What had happened? "Priya, let's go in and see," she whispered.

"No, let's stay here just a minute more," said Priya.

Just then they saw Santosh come out of the store room, where Ajji normally slept, turn into the main living room and walk towards the front door. He slipped on his chappals, took out his keys, and went out the front door.

Had he and Sharmila had a fight? Aruna wondered. Had she changed her mind about marrying him?

Then they heard Santosh calling them. "Priya! Aruna! Where are you?"

They ran around front to meet him.

"There you are! I heard you asking for a ride. Shall

we go?"

"What happened, Santosh?" Priya asked. "I heard Ajji crying."

"Nothing. Come, I'll take you for ice cream." He wheeled his motorcycle out the gate and onto the road.

"Santosh, you never take me for ice cream!" Priya protested. "What happened? Is everything all right?"

"Everything will be fine when we get back. Vandana is simply upset, that is all." He helped them onto the back of his motorcycle, then got on himself. "Hold tight!" he said, and they swerved off down the road in a roar. Aruna held tightly to Priya, who held on to Santosh. The wind whipped Aruna's hair into her face. Every time they turned a corner, the motorcycle tilted so much that Aruna was afraid she'd fall off. She clutched Priya harder and tried not to scream. Priya laughed — she wasn't afraid at all.

Finally they stopped at a little restaurant with two rickety green tables inside. At the counter Aruna ordered mango ice cream, Priya chose tutti-frutti, and Santosh had pistachio. They sat at a table and ate their ice cream while a little fan blew warm air at them.

"Come on Santosh, tell us," Priya pleaded as they ate. "At least say if it's serious or not. I don't want to worry for nothing."

"Why should you worry?" asked Santosh with a laugh. "You're only a child. You try to act too grown-up, Priya. Look at Aruna, how quiet and modest she is, even though she is from America."

Aruna looked up, surprised at this praise. She was quiet because she was afraid she might say something rude by mistake, or sound silly with her American drawl -- not because she was modest. Priya ignored Santosh's advice and kept pleading her case. Finally, she wore him down.

"Vandana has decided to go on a hunger strike," he said.

"Ayyo, but why?" Priya asked.

"Why does anyone go on a hunger strike? To get what she wants."

"But what does she want?"

"That you will have to ask Vandana."

Santosh would say no more no matter how much Priya begged, and they went home with their curiosity unsatisfied.

Chapter 13

*T*wo days had passed. Vandana was shut up in the store room, refusing to come out or eat. Everyone tiptoed around and whispered about what to do. At every mealtime, Ajji or Sharmila or Padma Auntie would take a plate of food in to Vandana to try to tempt her to eat. Ajji made Vandana's favorite foods — lemon rice with peanuts, and masala dosa. Ramesh Uncle brought home sweet orange mangos, creamy yellow guavas, and pomegranates with brilliant red jewel-like seeds. Aruna and Priya feasted on the fruits, but Vandana refused to eat anything. Ajji was so upset that she refused to eat anything either.

No one would tell Aruna or Priya what Vandana was upset about. In fact, no one paid much attention to the kids at all. They hung around the house and played games to pass the time till something happened. Finally, Priya decided they should visit Vandana themselves and ask her what was going on.

They waited till the adults were taking afternoon naps or watching an old movie on TV. Then they crept quietly to the store room door. Priya knocked softly, then pushed open the door when Vandana said "Who is it?" in Kannada.

They found her lounging in a chair that had been wedged into the tiny room, reading her feminist magazine, *Manushi*. Next to her on the floor was a steel pitcher of water, and a steel cup.

"Vandana, what is going on?" Priya got right to the point. She and Aruna sat on the rolled-up beds that Vandana and Ajji spread on the floor at night.

"I am on a hunger strike," Vandana stated, looking up from her magazine.

"That we know. But why? Nobody will tell us."

"I'll tell you. They won't let me study what I want. And they keep trying to show me all sorts of boys and have me paraded in front of them. Yesterday both your mothers gave me a long lecture, with the same old arguments — I will regret not marrying while I still look young, I must set a good example so you girls will also get married without fuss. My parents are growing old and want to see me married off so I will be taken care of if something happens to them. As if I can't take care of myself!" Vandana slapped the arm of her chair indignantly.

"When I find a man I like and respect, then only I will marry," Vandana continued. "I don't need someone else to find a husband for me." She took a sip of water from the steel cup beside her chair.

Aruna was surprised at Vandana's words. She had the impression that all Indians thought arranged marriage was good. But Vandana didn't like it! How confusing.

Vandana said, "It doesn't matter to anyone that I don't want to marry now. I've been studying anthropology, and I want to do field work in the Andaman and Nicobar islands. Father is absolutely against it, and so is your father, Priya."

"Ayyo, Andaman and Nicobar!" Priya sucked in her breath. "So dangerous for ladies, Vandana! How could you?"

"Priya, you have already become just as silly as all the other girls. Who told you it was dangerous? It's not at all. One must simply take the proper precautions, that's all."

"Vandana, they will not let you go," Priya declared. "You will only ruin your health if you don't eat."

"We'll see."

"But Vandana, how long can you keep this up? You will make yourself ill!" Priya jumped up and grabbed Vandana's arm. "I can't stand to think you will be ill. Why can't I bring you some food? I won't tell anyone." Priya whispered this suggestion to Vandana.

"Absolutely not. Someone is bound to find out with so many people around."

Priya tried to persuade Vandana with promises of absolute stealth and secrecy, but Vandana wouldn't budge.

"Go on! You are irritating me, Priya," she said.

"Then how can we help you?" Priya pleaded.

"First you can stop saying the islands are dangerous."

"But why do you want to go? There is nothing but prisons and tribal people who will shoot you with arrows."

"Not true. Some tribal people are hostile because first the British and then the Indian government cut down their trees and brought disease to the islands. I would be going there to study the culture, not destroy it. Therefore, they will not be hostile to me."

Priya kept trying to persuade Vandana to give up her fast, until Vandana finally ordered them out of the room and shut the door.

They wandered into the back yard and sat on a bench near the banana tree. Priya took hold of a banana leaf and started peeling it into sections absently. "What to do?" she muttered. "Why can't she be sensible?"

Aruna thought it would be really neat to go to an island and live with tribal people. "Where are these islands?" she asked.

"Out in the Bay of Bengal. Quite far away."

"Are they part of India?"

"Of course!" Priya looked at her incredulously. "I learnt all about them last year. Didn't you?"

Aruna shook her head, embarrassed by her ignorance.

Just then they heard their names being called.

"Priya! Aruna! Come here!"

They scrambled up and ran into the house. Santosh was in the main living room, with Priya's little brother Madhusudan. All the kids were going to the science and technology museum. Sharmila, Ajji, Padma Auntie and Aruna's mom were going to consult an astrologer to figure out what to do about Vandana.

Aruna and Priya bumped and sputtered along in the autoriksha to the museum, behind the auto that held Santosh and Madhusudan. Priya was so worried that she didn't say a word the entire trip. Aruna was worried too, but for a different reason. She was afraid that Vandana wouldn't get to do what she wanted. Aruna couldn't imagine being courageous enough to go on a hunger strike. She hoped she would never have to.

They shuffled into the museum and wandered from one echoing white room to another.

When they came to one room Aruna's interest picked up. It was devoted to specimens of rocks! She peered into a glass case and saw shiny reddish copper and nuggets of gold.

Santosh called them over to one particular case. "Look at this! My brother is a geologist, and this is what he mines." Aruna saw a silvery-white metal. "It's called manganese," Santosh explained. "It is combined with steel to increase the hardness and strength of the steel."

"Your brother is a geologist?" Aruna asked with interest. "What does he do?"

"He is a drilling manager at the manganese mines."

"I want to be a geologist, but I'm not going to mine anything," Aruna declared. "I'm going to identify rocks."

Santosh laughed. "How many rocks are there left to be identified? Everyone knows what they are. If you want to be a geologist, you have to be in mining. Look over there, at the model of the Kolar Gold Fields mine."

They went to look at a miniature replica of a scaffolding-like structure with tiny men working around it. Aruna thought it looked horribly industrial. She wanted to be an explorer — she wanted to wander around mountains and canyons, carrying her tools with her. "I don't want to work on something like that," she said.

"Mining is not a good profession for ladies," Santosh informed them. "You would be away from home in camps, mixing with all sorts of uneducated men. If you are good at science, better to take up medicine. That way you can set up a clinic in your own house."

Aruna didn't want to be a doctor. She couldn't stand to look at even the *picture* of the heart and lungs in the encyclopedia. Why did everyone want all Indian kids to be doctors? She wanted to be a geologist. "What else can a geologist do besides mining?" she asked.

"Nothing," said Santosh. "You must mine gold or manganese or diamonds, or work in the oil industry finding oil."

Aruna knew she didn't want to do that — tear up the earth to extract large quantities of something. If that was what a geologist did, maybe she shouldn't be a geologist after all. Anyway, it was kind of silly for a grown girl like her to be interested in rocks. No other girls in school thought rocks were interesting. She should probably try to be interested in something else.

She dragged herself through the rest of the museum and was glad when they got into the autorikshas for the ride home.

Chapter 14

Sharmila's wedding was only two days away. And Vandana still would not eat. Aruna and Priya were not sure what the astrologer had said about Vandana, but there were lots of closed-door meetings in the house. That morning a doctor had been brought in to examine Vandana.

Aruna was wandering around aimlessly in the afternoon. Everyone else was either taking a nap or watching a Hindi movie on TV at Priya's house. Since Aruna couldn't understand Hindi, she didn't feel like watching.

She walked in the back door of the main house. She thought she would read a book in the bedroom. But as she passed Vandana's door, which was open, she heard her name being called.

"Aruna! Come in here and keep me company," Vandana said.

Aruna stepped into the dim room. She liked Vandana and was glad to spend time with her. A portable fan whirred near the window, since this room had no ceiling fan. Vandana was sitting in her chair. She looked a little tired, but still cheerful. From a radio on the floor came the soft twanging sounds of a veena playing classical Indian music.

Aruna sat down on a bed roll and smiled at Vandana. "How do you feel?"

"I'm quite well, actually," Vandana said. "I can probably keep this up for some time."

Aruna admired Vandana's will-power. Aruna herself hated to be hungry. She wasn't sure what to say next. She certainly didn't want to talk about food. Or Sharmila's wedding, since Vandana didn't want to get married. What else should she say?

Vandana broke the silence. "How do you like your visit to India, Aruna?"

"I like it a lot!" Aruna said.

"What do you like about it?" Vandana persisted. "Don't you find life here too difficult? We have no air-conditioning, and no soft mattresses, and you must find everything smaller and dirtier than in the U.S."

Aruna agreed that was all true. "But I like all the people to talk to and play with. There are so many fun things to do!"

"Is that right?" Vandana said. She looked thoughtful for a moment. "Do you feel accepted in the U.S.? Is there a lot of racism against Indians there?"

"My dad said in his university sometimes, they don't

like to promote foreigners to high positions," Aruna replied. "But I don't notice anything in my school. I just wish I didn't look Indian. That's the first thing everyone notices about me. But I don't feel different inside. I feel like I'm just like the other kids. A lot of times I wish we could just be a normal American family."

Vandana laughed. "What is normal?" she asked. "I thought America was the land of diversity, the melting pot! How can there be just one type of normal?"

"But my family is *so* different," Aruna insisted. "We aren't even close to being normal."

Vandana laughed again. "I'm going to tell you something." She took a sip of water. "When I was a girl, I wished just the opposite. I wished our family could be a little abnormal. I thought we were too normal and boring."

Aruna furrowed her brow at Vandana. "Why would you want to be abnormal?"

"I thought it would be more interesting," Vandana said, smiling. "I had a friend at school who's mother was British. When I went to her house for tea they didn't serve Indian snacks. They had scones and jam. I thought it was great! And I had another friend who's mother was a local politician. My friend hated that — she wanted her mum to stay home cooking dosas or something. But to me it was so interesting."

Aruna realized something. "That's just what my best friend Darcy is always saying!" she exclaimed.

"What's that?" Vandana asked.

"Darcy has the perfect American family. She has a dog, and her mom bakes pies, and everything. But she says her family is boring. She came with me to Indian Sunday school once and she said it was so interesting! She liked it *because* it was different."

"There you go," Vandana said. "What you think is a disadvantage, someone else thinks is an advantage."

Aruna wasn't completely convinced. She didn't like to stand out and look different no matter how interesting someone else thought it was. She sighed. "I wish. . . I wish we could be just a *little* boring," she said.

Vandana was silent. She patted her hand on her knee in time to the veena on the radio. Finally she said, "If you are so unhappy in the U.S., why don't you ask your mum if you can live with us in India?"

Aruna stared at Vandana for a few seconds. Live in India? She had never thought about that possibility. Could she . . . would her parents allow it? And more importantly, would she like living in India, with Priya and Vandana and her grandparents? Would she feel like she belonged? Of course, there was her American accent — as soon as she opened her mouth everyone would know she was not normal. Maybe in time that would disappear.

Aruna decided she wanted to think about this possibility some more. She didn't think her parents would allow it, but it was interesting to consider.

◇   ◇   ◇

Later that afternoon, Aruna sat on the bed in their bedroom. She held a notebook in her lap, and she was carefully copying the Kannada script from an open book in front of her.

Before Aruna could decide whether she wanted to live in India, she thought she should see how hard it was to learn to write an Indian language. Priya had been learning to read and write Kannada and Hindi for years, in addition to English. So far Kannada was pretty hard — full of strange circles and swirls — but a lot of things were hard to learn at first.

Just then her mother walked in. "What are you doing here all alone, Aruna?" She opened one of the suitcases that were against the wall and started rummaging around in it for something.

Aruna held up the Kannada book. "I'm learning Kannada!" she said.

Mom found a hanky and tucked it into her sari. "That's good. Who gave you the idea to do that?"

"I did. Vandana told me that maybe I could live in India, so I decided to start learning Kannada. And Priya gave me the book."

Mom looked at Aruna for a few seconds. "You would like to live in India?" she asked quietly.

"Maybe. I haven't decided yet." Aruna waited for her mother's reaction, but Mom just stood there and stared at her. So she added, "Could I stay here if I wanted?"

Mom sat down on the bed beside Aruna. "I didn't

know you liked India so much! Before we left you were crying because you didn't want to come here."

"I know. But now I like it."

Mom gazed at Aruna. Then she smiled and squeezed Aruna's knee. She almost looked like she was going to cry. "If you really want to, I am sure we can arrange something," Mom said, her voice a little husky.

Aruna was surprised that her mother was willing to let her live in India by herself. "Would you miss me if I stayed here?" Aruna asked.

"Of course," Mom said. "But I could stay with you for a long time — maybe six months at a time. Some of my friends have done that."

"But what about Dad? Won't he be lonely in Ohio all by himself?" Aruna was getting worried at her mother's reaction.

"We'll see what Daddy will say," Mom said. She kept smiling at Aruna, and there were tears in her eyes.

Aruna suddenly saw her life in India stretch before her. She wouldn't be going sightseeing or shopping or visiting relatives all the time, like she was now. Every day she would have to walk the dusty streets with Priya to school. And every afternoon she would have to be tutored in languages, Indian geography and history, and who knew what else. At first she would be lonely because she wouldn't have any friends in her class. She would have to be polite and neat all the time, because she would always be a guest.

And after Aruna managed to learn everything, make

friends, and finish college, she would have an arranged marriage. That might not be so bad — Sharmila seemed to like it. But if she didn't want an arranged marriage, she might have to go on a hunger strike like Vandana.

It was too much to think about right now. Aruna closed the Kannada book and stood up.

"I will talk to Daddy," Mom assured Aruna, who nodded and ran out the door to find out what Priya was up to.

Chapter 15

*I*t was the morning of Sharmila's wedding. Sharmila, Ajji and Padma Auntie had been at the wedding hall since the night before. Now Priya and Aruna were taking baths, getting dressed, and deciding what jewelry to wear. Aruna wore her red and gold skirt and blouse, her mom's pearl and red stone necklace, and her own new bangles and bird earrings.

And — Vandana was going to the wedding too! She had given up her fast and eaten a meal the previous evening — just yogurt and rice, but food nevertheless.

"What happened?" Aruna asked her mom.

"I don't know," Mom brushed her off. "Don't ask so many questions."

Priya had not had any luck getting information from her mother, either. So after both girls were dressed, they went straight to Vandana to find out the truth.

They found her in the storeroom, in her slip and

bra, two saris folded on the shelf in front of her.

"Which shall I wear, girls?" she asked, pointing to a green and gold sari and a purple and silver sari.

"First tell us what happened, Vandana!" Priya insisted. "Are you going off to Andaman and Nicobar?"

"No — not yet," Vandana said regretfully, but with a smile. "But Father has agreed I don't need to get married now, and he will allow me to continue my studies in anthropology. So I thought that was as much as I could hope for now. I'll try for the field work later."

"Vandana, you really scared them!" said Priya. "Otherwise they wouldn't have changed their minds."

"Not only did I scare them, but the astrologer did too. It seems he told them if they got me married now, my husband would be very mean. He said best to let me study. And then of course he collected a large sum to perform all sorts of poojas so I would avoid bad luck!" Vandana laughed. "If they are all silly enough to waste their money on an astrologer, at least he did me a good turn."

Vandana chose the green and gold sari. Priya and Aruna sat and watched her wrap and pleat it around herself. Then they all sat in the front room to wait for Ramesh Uncle to take them to the wedding hall.

As she sat and waited, Aruna remembered that she had finally received a letter from Darcy the day before. She wanted to read it again. She ran into the bedroom, took the letter out of her suitcase, and sat on the floor. It was written on stationery from "Happy Valley Camp."

Dear Aruna,

How are you? I am fine. It is time to write letters at camp now, and I am writing to you. I got your letter at home. My mom sent it to me here. Wow, I wish I was with you! And I wish you were here too. Camp is fun. I get to sleep on the top bunk of the bed. The girls in my cabin are OK. One girl is totally afraid of everything, even swimming and everything fun, and she cries all the time. The horse that I ride is named Bridget and she's not very big. She's brown. I can almost gallop with her now. And we go swimming every day. The food is terrible here, except that every night we have a campfire and we roast hot dogs and marshmallows, so that's good. The camp counselors are really nice. That's all I can think of. See you in school!

Your friend,
Darcy

Aruna looked at the picture of the smiling sun and the words "Happy Valley Camp" on Darcy's letter. Darcy and camp and America seemed so far away — almost unreal. Aruna hadn't eaten a hot dog or marshmallows in so long.

Now that Aruna had been in India for a while, she had started to feel really comfortable. She didn't mind sleeping on a thin mattress. She didn't mind taking a bath with a bucket of water, instead of using a shower. She no longer rubbed off her kumkum with her hand by mistake. She liked wearing strings of jasmine flowers in her hair, and chappals, and even skirts. And she *really* liked having so many people around to hang out with.

But reading Darcy's letter also made her realize that she missed her friends at school. If she stayed in India, she would never be able to go to camp with Darcy and ride a horse. She wished she hadn't told her mother that she wanted to live in India. Somehow the news had gotten around fast — her mother had apparently told all her relatives, and now everyone was smiling at Aruna a whole lot and exclaiming, "So you will be staying with us!" It made a shiver go up Aruna's spine.

"Aruna! Let's go!" She heard Priya's voice calling her. She stuffed Darcy's letter back into the suitcase and ran out the front door. Ramesh Uncle's car was rumbling in the driveway, and they all piled in.

The big wedding hall was still empty, with a cool breeze blowing through it. Aruna saw a woman drawing rangoli with colored chalk on the ground in front of the hall, and inside the hall other people set up folding chairs for the guests to sit on.

They all went into one of the small rooms which lined one side of the hall. Inside, Sharmila sat in her slip and sari blouse, getting her hair made into a jasmine braid. "Beautiful!" murmured Aruna's mom. "Aruna, would you like to have your hair done like this?"

Sharmila's long braid and the back of her head were completely covered with neat rows of creamy jasmine flowers and another kind of orange flower that Aruna couldn't pronounce. The room smelled of warm sunshine and the perfume of jasmine.

"Is my hair long enough?" asked Aruna.

"They can attach a hairpiece," Priya informed her. "But you must sit very still when they put the flowers on."

Sharmila's hands and nails were decorated with delicate orange designs from mehendi. One of Sharmila's friends had come to the house a few nights before to apply the mehendi paste. Aruna and Priya had gotten their hands decorated too. You had to let the mehendi dry on your hands and sleep very carefully with it all night. And then when you peeled off the dried mehendi in the morning — your nails were orange and your hands had orange designs on them!

Aruna thought she preferred having mehendi on her hands, to having a jasmine braid — she could see her hands and enjoy the designs, but she wouldn't be able to see her own jasmine braid.

The wedding took all morning, but it was fun because no one except Sharmila and Santosh and the priest were expected to sit still in one place. Ajji and Thatha and Santosh's parents also had to sit with them for part of the ceremony. They all sat on a low platform on the floor facing the guests. There was a canopy above them, decorated with garlands of flowers.

Sometimes Aruna and Priya watched as the priest droned Sanskrit prayers. In front of him were whole brown coconuts, some type of leaves, small brass containers of raw rice, red kumkum powder, yellow turmeric powder, jasmine flowers, burning incense sticks, and Aruna didn't know what else.

Sharmila wore a yellow silk sari, gold necklaces, earrings, bangles, and even jewels in her hair. She looked beautiful, Aruna thought. Santosh wore a white silk dhoti and no shirt — just a silk shawl around his shoulders. At one point Sharmila and Santosh stood up, threw raw turmeric-colored rice over each other's heads, and put thick pink and white flower garlands on each other. Everyone laughed and exclaimed "ooh!" and "aah!"

Aruna and Priya also went outside to watch the musicians, dark skinny men playing a loud reedy instrument and drums, or back to the huge kitchen to watch the cooking. That's where they were, watching a wrinkled woman frying vadays in a vast pot of oil, when they heard their names being called.

"Aruna! Priya! Come quickly. They are putting the necklace on now!" Aruna's mom ushered them back into the wedding hall so they wouldn't miss the most important part of the ceremony. This event must occur at a certain time determined by an astrologer. Some people were even married in the middle of the night, because that was the luckiest time for them.

Sharmila wore a different sari now — a pink one.

Her cheeks were flushed and her eyes sparkled. "Santosh's parents gave her that sari after Sharmila was given away to Santosh," Aruna's mom explained. Aruna didn't like the idea that Sharmila was "given" to Santosh but he was not "given" to her.

Santosh held a gold pendant on a cotton cord. Sharmila was already wearing another similar pendant given to her by her mother. After the wedding both pendants would be put on a gold chain. That was the wedding necklace Sharmila would always wear.

Padma Auntie and Ajji bent over the necklace, fiddling with the cord and trying to get it untangled. With the help of Padma Auntie and Ajji, Santosh got the necklace tied around Sharmila's neck. There was no necklace for her to put on him.

Now they were married. But Sharmila and Santosh did not kiss. They just looked at each other and smiled.

For the next part of the ceremony a small fire was built in front of Sharmila and Santosh. "They will do pooja to Agni now, who is a witness to their marriage. They will promise to be good to each other," Aruna's mother explained.

Except for the excitement of seeing the fire, this part of the ceremony was long and boring. The priest would say a phrase in Sanskrit which Santosh and sometimes Sharmila had to repeat. Occasionally, Santosh would pour a little ghee into the fire.

Aruna and Priya made their way back to the kitchen.

Aruna was really hungry! She wondered when they would eat. Just then the wrinkled woman cook came up to them with a banana leaf on which were two fresh vadays. "Do you want these?" she asked in Kannada. She smiled indulgently at them. Aruna noticed her teeth and lips were red from chewing betel nuts and leaves. A few teeth were missing.

"OK." Priya accepted the banana leaf.

"Is the wedding over?" the woman asked.

"No," Priya replied. "They are still doing Agni pooja."

"Mm," the woman said. She watched silently as Aruna and Priya bit into the vaday, which were deliciously crisp on the outside and soft on the inside. "The husband and wife are both fair and tall," the woman observed approvingly. "Is it your sister?" she asked Priya.

"No, my aunt."

"You are also very pretty," she said, pinching Priya's cheek.

Priya swatted her hand away. "Go away!" she said rudely. The woman didn't seem offended, but just smiled and walked away. Aruna had noticed that the rule of being polite to elders didn't apply to servants. Aruna felt sorry for the thin, wrinkled woman who had so kindly brought them a snack.

The rest of the day went well. There was a big lunch, with guests sitting at rows of tables in the dining hall and a large piece of banana leaf displayed before each person.

Those were the disposable plates. Men servers with bare chests came around to serve everyone mounds of mushy white rice, rasam, sambar, various vegetable curries, vaday soaked in spicy yogurt, mango and lemon hot pickles, and sandigay, which looked sort of like pieces of styrofoam and tasted light and crispy and salty. Dessert was something Aruna loved: chiroti. It was a round, puffy, flaky pastry topped with powdered sugar. Aruna crumbled it on her banana leaf like everyone else did. Then a server poured sweet warm milk flavored with saffron and cardamom over it. Aruna thought it tasted kind of like an American breakfast cereal, only the milk was warm.

In the evening was the reception, also held in the hall. Santosh wore a suit and shoes, and Sharmila wore a very flashy orange sari covered with gold embroidery, and lots of makeup. Her blouse had puffed sleeves — the latest style. They sat on a sofa on a platform at one end of the hall. Aruna and Priya stood near the doorway and sprinkled the guests with rose water from special silver sprinklers as they walked into the reception. Aruna thought it was lots of fun — like using a squirt gun, except no one got upset.

Between guests, Priya confided in Aruna, "I want to marry someone just like Santosh. I will never make myself sick like Vandana. She looks so thin and dark today. Who will want to marry her?"

"She doesn't want to get married," Aruna pointed out.

"She will, soon," Priya said confidently. "Everyone

must get married. Even Shiva had to marry." Shiva was an ascetic god who shunned marriage. But the other gods convinced him to marry the goddess Parvati. So it did seem that everyone got married.

Aruna thought Priya was wrong. She thought there were men who would like Vandana, because she was — *interesting*. And who wanted to marry a man who only cared about your looks?

Chapter 16

Summer vacation was over already. Four big suitcases lay open on the bed and floor of the bedroom, and Mom sat amidst them, trying to fit all the clothes and crafts and gifts into them. Padma Auntie and Ajji kept bringing in boxes filled with Indian sweets, bags of spices, jars of pickles, and packages of dried sandigay.

Mom threw up her hands at every box or bag. "What is all this?" she said, laughing. "We do have food in America."

"You can't find good gooseberry pickles, you said, so take these."

Aruna also sat near a suitcase, packing. She was not going to stay in India — at least not now. It was too scary to think about making new friends. And even though she had managed to memorize the whole Kannada alphabet — over 50 characters in all — she hadn't made much progress at putting them together to form words.

Aruna thought it would be hard for her to fit in, in India.

First Aruna had told her decision to Vandana. "I'm going back. Maybe I'll even like being interesting," she said.

"That's right," Vandana said. "If you stay in the U.S. all your life you will always be a minority. People *will* see you as different, at least in the beginning. You must come to terms with that."

Then Mom broke the news to all the relatives. "So, you are going back to America," they said, patting Aruna on the back heartily. They didn't seem hurt that she didn't want to stay. "You can come back and live here for college," they assured her. And maybe she would.

But for now, Aruna would just have to be brave about looking different. After all, if Vandana could go on a hunger strike, couldn't she, Aruna, at least feel strong and happy to show her brown skin and black hair to the world?

Aruna had given some of her T-shirts to Priya. Now she had some new Indian tops decorated with embroidery, and two new cotton skirt and blouse outfits— a purple one and a peach-colored one — which she folded and laid in the suitcase. Wrapped neatly in a plastic bag was a magenta and bright green dancing outfit made especially for her, as well as a gold-colored metal belt that she would wear for dance performances.

Aruna tossed her new hairstyle back and forth as she packed. She had gotten a perm for her long hair, so now it was wavy instead of straight. And she had curly bangs now, just like Sharmila's. She couldn't wait to show off her hair at school.

She tucked the two silver and enamel bangles she had bought as a present for Darcy into a corner of her suitcase. Then she arranged a small stack of books over her clothes.

Her favorite among these books was a biography of a woman named Sarojini Naidu that Vandana had given her. Aruna gazed at the book's cover, which showed a fat, smiling gray-haired woman. Sarojini Naidu was the first Indian woman to work full-time in politics. She lived from 1879 to 1946, at a time when many Indian women were illiterate, but she went to college in England. She traveled all over India working for women's rights and India's freedom from British rule, and she also wrote beautiful poetry which was set to music.

As Aruna closed the book into her suitcase, she thought she might do a book report on that book if she got a chance. She was tired of avoiding books on India. After all, she should be able to read whatever she wanted!

◇   ◇   ◇

Aruna sat on a slippery plastic chair in the Bangalore airport and waited for their plane to be announced. Priya sat right next to her, holding her hand. Aruna didn't want to leave her relatives, especially her aunties. When would she see them again? Not for several years, at least.

She thought about what she would do when she got home. She wondered what mail she had gotten at home, and whether anything in their neighborhood would be changed when they got back. Probably some houses in the neighborhood would be finished. Maybe they would have some new neighbors already.

She was looking forward to starting seventh grade at the big junior high school. There would be a lot more kids there than at her elementary school. She made a promise to herself that she wouldn't talk about her rock collection. She didn't want to start off on the wrong foot again.

As they sat there waiting to board the plane, Aruna remembered the days she and Priya had spent at Santosh's family's house, where Sharmila lived now. That was fun. Sharmila's mother-in-law was always smiling and telling funny stories. She let Sharmila, Aruna and Priya cook all sorts of new recipes from magazines. Aruna and Priya went with Sharmila to her class on Japanese flower-arranging, and out shopping to buy vegetables. Sharmila had quit her job at the bank for now, until she got "settled in" to her new life.

Santosh went to work every morning, but came home for lunch. Sharmila served him lunch and sat with him while he ate. Aruna noticed that they hardly said anything to each other while Santosh ate — they just smiled at each other a lot. In the evenings, sometimes they all played cards or carrom. Other times Santosh would take them out for ice cream, or a movie. Priya was thrilled. "I can't wait to get married!" she said.

"It's not always like this, you know," warned Sharmila. "Santosh is only taking us out for your sake, not for me. When you are not around, all I do is work." She laughed and nudged Santosh, who nudged her back and said, "Listen to her! I work all day in a dull office, and she enjoys herself at home."

Vandana had visited over the weekends, and she was very glad to see that Santosh and his mother were so kind to Sharmila, and that Sharmila was happy in her new home.

Now all that fun was over. Aruna and her family would go back to their own house with just three quiet people in it — no aunts or cousins to chat with or play with.

The loudspeakers blared something incomprehensible, and Aruna's mom and dad stood and picked up the carry-on bags. Padma Auntie and Vandana hugged Aruna. Then Aruna's family stepped through the security gates alone, as the rest of the family watched. Aruna felt a lump in her throat and tears in her eyes. She didn't want to look back — she didn't want them to see her crying.

Chapter 17

"You have a letter from Vandana," Mom informed her as Aruna came home one day after school, about six weeks after they'd gotten back from India. "It's on the table by the couch."

Aruna threw her books on the couch and picked up the blue Indian airmail letter, with an intricate purple stamp of a bird with curlicue feathers.

Aruna liked being home, and being able to sleep in her own bed and eat whatever she wanted and not have to look out for cockroaches. She liked turning on the TV or radio and always being sure she would understand the language. She was starting to think Vandana was right — she *was* more American than Indian. Even if she *looked* like a foreigner in the U.S., she *felt* like a foreigner in India.

But she also missed India. When they'd first gotten back to the U.S., the house seemed so hushed. It was strange to wake up in her room by herself, and not to have

Ajji or Padma Auntie giving her a hot cup of milk as soon as she woke up.

She was glad to get a letter. So far, seventh grade had been disappointing. She and Darcy were in completely different sections of the big junior high school, and they didn't have any classes together. They saw each other only at lunchtime. Aruna's heart sank when she found out that Emily and Amber were in the same section as she was.

The first day of school, Aruna had appeared at the bus stop with her new hair style, wearing one of her new Indian embroidered tops over her jeans. When Amber and Emily walked up to her she smiled and said, "Hi!"

Emily had on a very short mini skirt. Amber wore a tight pair of jeans, and she didn't pull her red hair back in a ponytail anymore. She let it loose, and had somehow made it full and puffy on top. Both girls wore make-up: Emily wore pale pink lipstick, and Amber wore a gold-colored lipstick.

Amber stopped in front of Aruna and looked her up and down. "You look like you just got out of bed. Is that a pillowcase you're wearing?" She and Emily burst out laughing, then flounced over to some 8th grade boys on the corner and started talking and giggling to them.

Aruna hugged her notebook closer to her chest to hide her new blouse. She could feel tears starting to form in her eyes, but she bit the inside of her cheek so she wouldn't cry. Did her blouse really look like a pillowcase? It was white and sleeveless, kind of a rectangular top, with embroidery at the neck. Aruna realized with horror that it did sort of look like an embroidered pillowcase! She vowed never to wear her new Indian tops again.

Just then, out of the corner of her eye, Aruna saw a new girl standing at the bus stop. It was another Indian girl — someone she recognized from Sunday school! Her name was Leena and Aruna remembered Mom saying that Leena's family had just moved into their neighborhood. Leena smiled shyly at Aruna from behind her books. She had long straight hair that hung down her back, just the way Aruna's used to be. Aruna smiled back, but she was too embarrassed to say anything. Had Leena seen how Amber and Emily laughed at her?

That very day, Aruna had written Vandana a long letter telling her all about the mean girls who laughed at her, even though she had a new hairstyle and new clothes. "I'm too babyish. That's why they laughed at me," she wrote. She also told Vandana she had decided to throw out her rock collection. She was too mature for that kind of thing now, and she wasn't ever going to be a geologist anyway since she didn't want to be a miner. She told her mom the same thing.

"Don't throw those rocks in the yard," Mom warned. "I don't want to have your rocks in my garden. Throw them somewhere else."

She hadn't yet figured out where to dispose of them, so they were still sitting in the basement gathering dust when she got Vandana's letter.

She sat down on the couch, carefully sliced open the air letter and spread it on her lap.

"My dear Aruna," the letter began.

I am sorry to hear that your new school is not a success. It must be very hard for you to have some girls laugh at you simply because of the clothes you wear. I know you may not believe me, but don't worry about those girls. In 10 years' time, if they do not change their ways, they will be bitter and unhappy women.

But Aruna, I am truly more worried because you say you will do away with your rock collection. What you write makes me sad. You must not give up your dream just because a few people laughed at it.

When I was a child so many people laughed at me because I was interested in anthropology and the different customs and traditions throughout India. Most of my relatives told me that our family's customs were the best, and why did I want to study somebody else's tradition, since those other traditions were inferior, after all?

If I had given up my ideas, I would not now be studying this fascinating subject. I feel that through my future work I may really be able to help Indians get over their prejudices against people of other castes and customs. This is important in In-

dia, where so many people are illiterate and so much violence is caused because people misunderstand the customs of other people.

Aruna, by trying to please everyone you will please no one. Most people in this world follow the herd. They are not courageous enough to do anything different.

You say you do not want to be a miner. There are many other things you can do as a geologist besides mining. For example, you can study volcanoes or earthquakes. Or you can identify fossils and be a paleontologist. Why don't you go to the library and research all the different things a geologist can do?

Please, keep your rocks. You must not give up something that you have worked so hard on just because a few others laugh. I want to see your collection when I come to the U.S. someday. Write to me soon.

Yours affectionately,
Vandana

Aruna continued to stare at the letter in her lap after she'd read it. Ten years' time! That seemed forever for Emily and Amber to get their due. In the meantime, would they keep laughing at her?

Aruna sighed, and refolded the letter. Then she

went down to the basement to look at her rock collection.

She carried her box of rocks to an old carpet remnant on the cement floor, underneath the light bulb, and sat down. She always loved to look at her rocks. She picked up each one and dusted it off, remembering where she had found it.

Her best rocks were two chunks of cloudy quartz — one white, one pink — that she'd picked up outside their motel in South Dakota, when they went to see Mount Rushmore. She rubbed their glossy translucent surfaces. On that same trip she'd also found a dime-sized piece of golden mica, about 1/4 inch thick — big enough so she could actually distinguish the thin, transparent layers that made it up.

She also had a large piece of conglomerate — pebbles stuck together with sediment — and some sandstone, slate, pink and white granite, and other common rocks. She had an incomplete arrowhead emerging from a small piece of black flint, found near the woods behind the apartments where they used to live. She had a neat piece of mica schist too — mica that had metamorphosed after high pressure or high temperature into a dense, glittery gold rock.

Finally, Aruna picked up the small, battered crystal that she thought was gypsum. She remembered how her friends at her old school had inspected it. So not all girls laughed at rock collections. Aruna slipped the crystal into her pocket. She would show it to Darcy the next day at

lunch. She had never shown Darcy any of her rocks before, but she knew Darcy would appreciate them.

Darcy loved the silver and enamel Indian bangles
Aruna had given her — she wore them all the time, and no
one made fun of her. Who cared about stupid old Amber
and Emily? Aruna thought maybe she would go ahead and
wear her Indian tops. She should be able to wear whatever
she wanted.

In fact — Aruna felt ambition spark through her —
tomorrow she would wear her beautiful purple skirt and
blouse outfit from India, which she had never worn at all.

She had been sitting so long on the floor bending
over her box that her neck was getting stiff. She stood up
and carried her rock collection back to the shelf. She figured she may as well keep it, especially since Vandana
wanted to see it someday.

Besides, Vandana said geologists could study volcanoes and fossils, and Aruna certainly liked learning about
volcanoes and fossils. Maybe Santosh was wrong — maybe
there were other things a geologist could do besides mining. She would have to find out.

Chapter 18

*A*runa blinked her eyes in the bright sunlight streaming through the window as she lay in bed. It looked warm outside! She threw off the covers, got out of bed, and opened the window.

A soft breeze wafted against her face. It was a beautiful day. The sky was blue, and the leaves on the big maple tree in their front yard were starting to turn bright red. Aruna breathed in the fresh, spring-like scent. She vaguely remembered that today she was going to do something different. Then her heart tightened and she realized — she had decided that today, she was going to wear her new Indian clothes. Today she was going to be *interesting*.

Now Aruna wondered whether she was going a little too far. Why spoil such a pretty day? Maybe today she should just wear her usual baggy T-shirt.

She ran into the bathroom to take her shower. Then, in her bedroom, she opened a dresser drawer and looked at a pile of T-shirts, most of them faded — just the way she liked.

Before she selected a T-shirt, she thought she might just look at her Indian tops. She could wear an Indian blouse with jeans today — that wouldn't be too bad. She opened the closet door. Near the back end of the closet she saw her Indian tops, including the white one that Amber said looked like a pillowcase. Among them was the purple outfit. Aruna lifted it out of the closet to look at. It was a rich, deep purple, with a soft gloss — cotton that looked almost like silk. The blouse had puffed sleeves, and delicate white flowers embroidered around the neckline. The skirt had white flowers all around the hem. She laid them on the bed. They were even prettier than she had remembered.

Before she could change her mind, she slipped the blouse over her head, and tied the skirt around her waist. Out of a carved sandalwood jewelry box on her dresser she took her new silver and amethyst earrings, and inserted them in her ears. And just before she left the house for the bus stop, she slipped her feet into a pair of black chappals.

Aruna held her books against her chest as she walked. What would Amber and Emily say today? Her skirt swished around her legs, and she could feel her crystal, as well as a few other stones, in the skirt pocket.

As she rounded the corner, she saw Emily and Amber giggling with the eighth-grade boys. Amber blinked her mascara-covered eyelashes at a skinny blond boy, and

Emily swung her hips as she talked to a skinny brown-haired boy. They didn't even seem to see Aruna as she walked by.

Aruna stood in the warm sun by herself and chewed her lip. She was early — still eight more minutes till the bus arrived. She should have waited at home, but she had been so eager to show off her new attitude. She had been prepared to retort something clever to Emily and Amber when they criticized her clothes. Of course, today no one cared.

She was aware of someone running towards them. She turned her head and saw a brown girl jogging to the bus stop — Leena, the new Indian girl in the neighborhood.

For the past month or so, Aruna had made careful plans to avoid speaking to Leena every morning at the bus stop. Most days she had dawdled, until the bus pulled up, at a pile of rubble around the corner, and pretended to look for rocks even though she already knew there was nothing interesting in that pile. Over the weeks she had been forced to say a few words to Leena, and she had found out that Leena's family had moved to the neighborhood in July, and that Leena had been waiting for Aruna to come back from India since then. Aruna felt wretched trying to avoid Leena. But she just couldn't bring herself to associate with another Indian girl — not in front of Amber and Emily, anyway.

As Leena neared, Aruna's heart beat faster. She took a deep breath, put on a friendly smile, and walked a few steps towards her. "Hi!"

"Hi," Leena said, panting as she ran up. She stood looking at Aruna for a few seconds, like she wasn't sure whether Aruna really meant to stick around and talk. Then she said, "I thought I was going to be late. Our kitchen clock must be fast."

"You're five minutes early," Aruna said.

They continued to smile at each other. Then Aruna said, "Do you like our school?" and Leena said at the same time, "Did you get that outfit in India?"

"It's OK," said Leena.

"Yes," said Aruna. Leena giggled. Aruna giggled too. Out of the corner of her eye she looked at Amber and Emily. What were they doing? Were they looking at her? But they were still absorbed with the boys.

Leena got on the bus first, and chose a seat near the middle — far away from Amber and Emily, who always sat at the very back of the bus. Aruna swung herself into the seat and sat down beside Leena. As the bus rumbled along, Leena asked,

"How was your trip to India?"

"It was fine," Aruna said. She didn't want to tell Leena how much she liked India — what if Leena hated India? But Leena kept looking at her so she said, "At first it was hard because it was so different. But then I got used to it."

Leena said, "We were in India last summer and I was so afraid to go to the bathroom for the first few days. I didn't want to squat down, you know, and use water. I didn't eat or drink anything, so I wouldn't have to go!"

Aruna was amazed. "How could you do that? You'd still have to go even if you didn't eat or drink."

"Well, I tried not to," said Leena. "But then I got used to India and I had so much fun. I didn't want to leave at all. My parents had to practically drag me out of the airport at the end of the summer."

Aruna stared at Leena. So that had happened to Leena too! She was surprised to know that someone else felt the same way about India that she did.

All day, Aruna had to keep reminding herself that today she was trying her new experiment. Sometimes it wasn't easy. In home room Aruna's teacher, Ms. Solomon, went into raptures about Aruna's outfit. "It's so unique!" gushed Ms. Solomon. "I really want to visit India some-day. You know, I watched every episode of that show on PBS, *The Mysteries of India.*" Aruna felt like staring at the ground and shuffling away, but she smiled politely and thanked Ms. Solomon.

Aruna could hardly wait for lunchtime, to show Darcy her rocks. As she put her lunch tray down next to Darcy's she was happy to see that Darcy was still wearing her Indian bangles. But then Darcy said, "I love your san-dals, Aruna!" She stood up to get a better look at Aruna's feet. "Are those from India? They are so cute! I wish I had a pair like those!"

Aruna started to wish that she had never worn her

chappals. But she remembered what she had talked about with Vandana — that Darcy was fascinated by things that were unusual. So she told Darcy, "You can borrow them sometime. But let's not talk about it now. I want to show you something else."

She was about to take her rocks out of her pocket to show Darcy, when her heart skipped a beat — she saw Leena standing at the front of the lunchroom holding her tray and looking around at the sea of faces. Leena looked confused and lost, just the way Aruna had felt last year at her new school.

"Wait a sec," Aruna told Darcy. She hurried up to where Leena stood and said, "Come sit with us." Leena's face broke into a smile as she followed Aruna to her table.

They sat down, and Aruna introduced Darcy and Leena. Aruna took a bite of pizza and a mouthful of wilted green beans. She felt very pleased with herself. It wasn't so hard to be interesting after all! Now she would really dazzle Darcy and Leena with her rocks.

Aruna laid her rocks on the lunch table — her two pieces of cloudy quartz, the mica, and the crystal. She looked at Darcy expectantly.

"What're those?" Darcy asked. She shoveled tapioca pudding into her mouth.

"These are my best rocks. From my rock collection," Aruna announced.

"Mm." Darcy continued to eat. Aruna looked at Leena, who smiled and said politely, "They're very nice."

Aruna could tell that Leena didn't think they were very nice at all.

Everyone was silent. Aruna stared at her rocks. They looked small and lonely sitting in the middle of the lunch table. Aruna's eyes started to mist over. Her experiment wasn't going well after all. She grabbed her rocks back and shoved them into her skirt pocket. Darcy continued to eat her pudding, and Leena was nibbling on her pizza.

Aruna didn't want to eat any more. She felt a lump in her throat. Why didn't Darcy like her rocks? Maybe no girls in the seventh grade liked rocks. Maybe that was just for elementary school girls.

As she sat there, not eating, Aruna thought about Vandana's letter. Vandana had said she wanted to see the rocks, and she was a lot older than seventh grade. Aruna drew out her rocks again. She took a deep breath and asked,

"Have you ever seen a rock that looks like paper?"

"Paper!" Darcy exclaimed. "What do you mean?"

"Look at this. It's called 'mica.'" She held it out for their inspection and with a fingernail, carefully loosened the top layer of the mica. She didn't want to take it off completely — it was a pretty small piece of mica and it could use every one of its layers — but she loosened it enough so they could see how thin and transparent it was.

"Wow, that's neat!" Darcy exclaimed. Leena also looked interested.

Then Aruna showed them the crystal. "Look, this

is a crystal. But it's so soft that you can scratch it with your fingernail."

Darcy immediately picked it up and wanted to scratch it. "Scratch it down low so you don't mess it up," Aruna suggested. Darcy did so and said, "What a strange crystal."

"It's called 'gypsum,' " Aruna said.

Leena was now holding Aruna's piece of light-pink rose quartz. "This is really pretty," she said — this time like she meant it.

Aruna was ready to put her rocks away now, but her friends were still busy examining and stroking them. Finally they were finished and Aruna said, "You can come over and look at the rest of my rocks too. And maybe we can go rock collecting together."

"I never knew rocks were so interesting," Darcy said. "I knew you had a rock collection, but you never told me what you liked about them. Rocks don't move or fly, like insects do. And they don't have strange or interesting habits, like a praying mantis or a honeybee. But I guess there's more to them than I thought."

Aruna was surprised at Darcy's words. She had just assumed that other people should be able to see the beauties of rocks, just as she herself did. But if even Darcy didn't understand until Aruna explained it — she realized she would have to talk about her rocks more.

At the end of the day, as she rode home on the bus with Leena, Aruna decided it had been a good day. Not exactly an easy day, but a good one.

The bus heaved to a stop near Aruna's house. She descended and waved goodbye to Leena — but not for long. Leena had asked her to come over later on to do their homework together, and Aruna had actually agreed. And that Saturday, she, Leena and Darcy were going to the field near Darcy's house to collect rocks and insects.

Aruna's chappals made a slapping sound against her heels with each step and her rocks felt heavy in her pocket. As she walked along, she realized she was glad she had decided to do what she wanted. She was glad she had decided to keep her rock collection. And she was glad she had ignored Emily and Amber and worn her new purple outfit. She couldn't wait to write to Vandana to tell her about her successful day.

Maybe, Aruna thought — maybe she was even becoming courageous — like Vandana!

She started grinning to herself at this thought. She gave a little skip, and soon she was running home, her hair flying behind her.

Glossary

Agni — the Hindu god of fire.

Ajji — grandmother (in the Kannada language).

autoriksha — a three-wheeled motorized vehicle for hire. Also called "auto."

aviyal — a coconut and vegetable curry.

ayyo — an exclamation, like "Oh!"

betel nuts and leaves — the nuts and leaves of a plant, which are often chewed after meals. They turn the teeth and lips red if chewed regularly.

Bhagavad Gita — a Hindu religious book. It involves a philosophical conversation between Prince Arjuna and Lord Krishna.

Bharata Natyam — a classical dance of southern India.

Brahmin — one of the four "castes" of traditional Indian society (see the entry on "caste").

carrom — a game, somewhat similar to pool, involving a board with four corner pockets. Players take turns shooting disks into the pockets.

caste — a traditional way to divide Hindus, according to the profession of the men in a family. There are four main castes: Brahmins, who were priests, and had the highest social status; Kshatriya, the warriors; Vaishya, people who sold goods and services for money; and Shudra, laborers. Even lower in status were the "untouchables," who performed work that others thought unclean — working with human and animal corpses. They were outside the caste system. Today, most people who live in Indian cities no longer follow the profession of their caste.

Many people in India have spoken out against the caste system, which discriminates against people of the "lower" castes and the "untouchables" (who prefer to be called "dalits" now, and whom Mahatma Gandhi called "harijan," or children of God.) It is illegal in India to discriminate based on caste. Yet many people, especially in rural areas, still cling to strict caste divisions.

chapati — a flat wheat bread.

chappals — Indian sandals.

dal — lentils or split peas. Many different kinds of lentils are used in Indian cooking.

dhoti — a garment worn by Indian men. It consists of a piece of cloth, usually white cotton, wrapped around the waist and legs.

Diwali — an important Indian holiday, which takes place at the end of October or the beginning of November. It is the "festival of lights." To celebrate, people light oil lamps, firecrackers, and sparklers, and receive new clothes.

dosa — a sourdough crepe. The batter (made of raw rice, lentils and water) is ground and allowed to ferment overnight. Then it is poured on a hot griddle to make a thin "pancake" or crepe.

Ganesha — a Hindu god with the body of a man and the head of an elephant. He is the god of wisdom and new beginnings.

ghee — a condiment made from butter that has been boiled, and the solids removed. Ghee does not need to be refrigerated, and is a way to preserve butter.

Hindi — one of the two official languages of India. It is spoken mostly in northern India. (The other official language is English).

jubba — an Indian tunic-top worn mostly by men.

Kannada — an Indian language spoken mostly in the state of Karnataka.

kumkum — the dot Hindu women wear on their forehead. Also called "bindi." It is traditionally applied with a red powder, but nowadays self-stick kumkum is available in many colors, shapes, and sizes.

Lakshmi — the Hindu goddess of prosperity.

Mahatma Gandhi — a famous Indian man who led the Indian struggle for independence from British rule during the first half of the 20th century. Gandhi pioneered the concept of "non-violence" as a way to pressure the British to leave. No weapons were used, but instead Indians boycotted British goods and defied British laws in order to force them to leave.

masala dosa — a sourdough crepe filled with potato curry.

mehendi — the henna plant. The leaves of this plant are used to dye hair and nails.

pachadi — a yogurt dish with cucumbers and spices. Also called "raita."

palya — a vegetable side-dish prepared dry, without sauce.

paisa — Indian coin. One-hundred paisa make up one rupee (see "rupee" below).

pooja — Hindu religious rituals.

poori — a deep-fried bread that puffs up into a ball when cooked.

prasada — food that is offered to God for blessings, then eaten.

raja — darling, or dear.

rangoli — sacred designs drawn on the ground in front of temples, homes, or wedding halls. They are drawn with chalk or with a white powder.

rasam — a lentil and tomato broth.

rupee — the basic Indian monetary unit.

salvar kameez — a traditional dress of Indian women, involving a pair of baggy pants and a knee-length tunic top.

sambar — a lentil and vegetable stew.

samosa — a vegetable turnover.

sandigay — a fried snack made of rice or wheat flour. The flour is boiled and made into a dough, then passed through a special press to form various shapes. These shapes are dried in the sun for a day or two, and stored until needed. Before eating, the sandigay is deep-fried in oil.

Sanskrit — an ancient language of India, in which many Hindu religious books are written.

sari — a traditional dress of Indian women, involving six or nine yards of cloth wrapped and pleated around the body. It is worn with a short blouse.

Thatha — grandfather (in the Kannada language).

vaday — a fried snack made of dal. The dal is soaked and ground, then mixed with spices, made into small patties, and deep-fried.

veena — a large stringed instrument of South India.

About the author:

Jyotsna Sreenivasan was born in Ohio in 1964, and lived most of her childhood in northeastern Ohio, with brief stints in Toronto, Canada and Bangalore, India. Her parents came to the United States from India in 1962. She has always loved to write, and earned her M.A. in English at the University of Michigan. She is also the author of another children's novel, *The Moon Over Crete*. She lives in Washington, DC with her husband. Her name is pronounced JOE-tsnah SHREE-nee-vah-sun.

About the illustrator:

Merryl Winstein is the sister-in-law of Jyotsna Sreenivasan. She has a B.F.A. in art from Washington University in St. Louis, Missouri, and has written and illustrated a book, *Your Fertility Signals*.

Write to the author!

Jyotsna Sreenivasan loves to hear from her readers. You can write to her at P.O. Box 15481, Washington, DC 20003-0481. If you would like a reply, please enclose a self-addressed, stamped envelope.